THE MIND OF DR. MORELLE

Borgo Press Books by ERNEST DUDLEY

The Amazing Martin Brett: Classic Crime Stories
Department of Spooks: Stories of Suspense and Mystery
More Cases of a Private Eye: Classic Crime Stories
The Private Eye: Classic Crime Stories
The Return of Sherlock Holmes: A Classic Crime Tale

THE DR. MORELLE CLASSIC CRIME SERIES

Dr. Morelle and the Doll: A Classic Crime Novel
Dr. Morelle at Midnight: A Classic Crime Novel
Dr. Morelle Investigates: Two Classic Crime Tales
Dr. Morelle Meets Murder: Classic Crime Stories
The Mind of Dr. Morelle: A Classic Crime Novel
New Cases for Dr. Morelle: Classic Crime Stories

THE MIND OF DR. MORELLE

A CLASSIC CRIME NOVEL

ERNEST DUDLEY

THE BORGO PRESS

MMXIII

THE MIND OF DR. MORELLE

*Special thanks to Heather and Dave Datta
for scanning this book.*

FIRST BORGO PRESS EDITION

Published by Wildside Press LLC

www.wildsidebooks.com

DEDICATION

For Matthew Sweet

CONTENTS

CHAPTER ONE

Through the deep waters shadowed by the huge rock headed the school of herring-fry, moving up to the surface in close-packed array.

The smooth sea lapped gently against the weed-fringed base of the rock, overhead herring gulls, alerted by the appearance of the fish below, swooped and wheeled through the warm air in greedy anticipation.

Then, as if in answer to some silent signal from the gulls, there shot out of the sea depths score upon score of bluefish, to drive like a steely arrow into the herring-fry, their sharp, murderous mouths working viciously. With electrifying speed the bluefish twisted and turned through the serried ranks of their prey, slashing and tearing, leaving behind them myriads of mangled corpses.

The sea swirled and threshed above the one-sided battle. Now, the herring gulls swooped with shrill cries to attack and devour the tattered remnants of the fish which began to scatter about the surface.

At this moment another menace appeared on the scene; suddenly from out of the sun, a flock of terns threw its swift shadow over the gulls, and circling while it sighted its objective, it dived like some massive suicide squadron to the attack. Their objective was the remaining herring-fry which swam aimlessly just beneath the surface of the swirling waters, seeking to escape the vicious attack of their adversary from below.

The air was a chaos of grating shrieks and angry cries from

the gulls as the tern plummeted down and then wheeled off with their crammed beaks, leaving the sea behind them a maelstrom. The bluefish, realizing the danger from above, changed course and disappeared into the depths shadowed by the great rock, leaving what remained of the herring-fry to make good their escape. Only a few tattered corpses now cluttered the sea for the gulls to select at their leisure.

It was the sight of several of the herring gulls, white and flashing against the blue sky, which attracted the attention of the man in the black hired car, he paused on the road beside the cliffs overlooking the expanse of water of Buzzards Bay, which sparkled in the late morning sunlight.

He made a stocky figure in his early forties. Though his face had run to seed a bit, he was still quite a handsome man. Except around the jaw. Even the excess flesh could not hide the weak chin. The eyes were bluish-grey, friendly, and calculating at the same time, a fine network of the lines of dissipation surrounding them.

He relaxed behind the wheel of the car, idly watching the gulls, and then he turned his gaze to the road ahead of him. The air was heavy with the scent of flowers, bayberry and beach-plum, and nearby junipers rustled in the gentle breeze that lifted off the sea. Ahead was a drive which ran between two rough granite posts. The man could see the white gate of locust timber swung back open for his arrival. Through the thin belt of trees, he could make out beyond the hedges several buttonwood trees, old and gnarled, and a short distance beyond them the house itself.

This was J.K's place. It was the first time he had seen it. He had caught a Northeast Airlines plane from New York to Hyannis that morning, and picked up the drive-yourself car at the airport. Now here he was, a mile the other side of Falmouth, whose typical houses built by Cape Cod captains, with herb gardens and everywhere roses, he had just driven through.

For a moment he watched a seaplane from Woods Hole head

across Buzzards Bay for Nantucket, then, his expression hardening a little, he let in the clutch. He reached the turning and drove past the granite posts, on to the drive of crushed oyster shell.

He stopped the car at the end of the drive where there was a paved brick courtyard. He got out of the car, stretching his short, thick legs. The air reverberated to the humming of bees in the hedges. The house before him was a sprawling, single-story, white-timbered building at the end of a mossy brick path. On either side of him as he slowly made his way along the path stretched lawns and flower gardens, woodbine and aster. To his right stood a rough granite barn, patched with green and yellow lichen, over whose roof sprawled masses of English ivy. Beside the barn lay several unmounted cannon, black and glinting dully, some incongruous relic of the Civil War, no doubt.

A ratbird sped across his line of vision, everywhere birds sang, and the breeze off the sea, which glittered through the trees on his right, was cool and refreshing. A faintly grim smile touched his face as he surveyed the scene. For a weekend haunt, or holiday laze-about, which was J.K's description of it to him, it didn't look too bad.

In front of him the shallow spreading salt-box roof of the house sloped from the central chimney stack to a gracefully pillared portico, underneath which the front doors stood wide open. As he went towards them he saw the sun terrace on his left which overlooked Buzzards Bay.

Beneath it ran a long, crazy-paved terrace, on which a long canopied hammock swung gently to and fro.

What had drawn his attention to the hammock was the pair of long, shapely legs, sunned to a light tan. Their owner was hidden by the gaily-striped back cloth of the hammock. But if the rest of her, he thought, looked anything like what he could see, J.K. was doing all right.

The double doors which opened as if expecting him were white painted, the upper halves glazed with panes of glass bull's-eyes. He stood there, taking in the cool interior, the white scrubbed floorboards, spread with rugs and mats, and the typical Cape Cod furniture, and miscellany of ships' wheels and sea charts, marine lamps and lanterns and ships' models, and a chipped figurehead in one corner. All the trimmings, he thought. Then a short, dark manservant, white-jacketed, suddenly appeared. He looked like a half-breed, probably mixed Portuguese and Indian blood, with narrow black eyes in a long face.

'Mr. Gale?' And Edwin Gale nodded and followed the other past the wide staircase. This was the heart of the house, this big, square-shaped room with windows everywhere, with the staircase and the great fireplace, full now with masses of flowering plants, and decorated with fans of coral and nautilus shells. An archway led to a floor of silverstone flagging, along which the man in front moved silently, while his own expensive shoes clicked loudly. He found himself dabbing his face with his handkerchief.

It had been a stifling heat in New York, but here at Cape Cod, which was a bent finger of land hooked into the Atlantic Ocean, the hot summer was tempered with a gentle salt-tanged air. Here at Falmouth, with its lovely beaches and historical streets, and here in this cool, sprawling house, he shouldn't have felt the heat the way he had in Manhattan. But he wasn't finding it cool at this moment. In spite of the loosely-cut summer-weight suit he was wearing, and the thin, soft shirt, he was sweating.

And that hadn't happened even in all the humidity since he had pulled off the deal. He knew it was nothing to do with the heat, it was to do with his mind and how J.K. affected it. J.K., who should have met him in New York instead of dragging him all this damned way to Cape Cod. Admittedly, J.K. was entitled to call the tune a bit; it was through him, and with his backing, that he'd so successfully put it over the wealthy old chump in Chicago.

There was no doubt J.K. was a smooth operator. He could pull the right strings at the right time. He always seemed to know where the body was hidden, all right. And all the time he himself stayed right in the background, unseen, unknown, unsuspected. Which was fine, from J.K's angle, if anything went wrong. He always got what he wanted. And what Gale was turning over, back of his mind, was the notion that he sometimes got more than he was entitled to. Over this deal, for instance, what was worrying him was that, now it was the time for the payoff, would he be asking for a bigger cut than arranged?

Gale thought he had heard it foreshadowed in the other's tone when he had called him up to fix that he should fly down to Cape Cod to see him to wind up all the business end, J.K's business end. It could be that this was what made him sweat in the coolness of J.K's sprawling, over-ornate house.

His mind was jerked back from his morbid ruminations by the manservant halting at a wide open door and turning to him with his uneven teeth drawn back in a little smile. The man stood aside; for a fleeting moment Gale felt as if he was being ushered like some fly into the spider's web.

He went into the room. It was a big room; the walls were of pine from floor to ceiling, mellowed by the years to a shade of old ivory. The ceiling was plaster, once white, but now like the walls tinted to a creamy colour, and divided into panels by adz-hewn oak beams. From the ceiling was suspended a magnificent chandelier of gleaming glass. The floor he was crossing was of very wide pine strips, painted black, speckled with white and tarnished yellow. In it was his own reflection and the furniture: the old chairs, the big table of birdseye maple. One end of the room was shelved, books packing the wall; running full-length of the wall on his left were two shelves, one above the other, full of glass. Flint glass, Sandwich lace glass, etched glass. There was blown glass and pressed glass: bowls, plates, decanters, pitchers and tumblers. The double array glinted and glittered fantastically, and caught the light of the morning sun which shafted in through the french windows, which filled almost all of the end of the room. Beneath this sparkling array lay a long sea chest with rope handles, decorated with paintings of ships and anchors, whales and mermaids.

In a corner of the room by the white-painted french windows

stood an enormous, carved sea captain's desk, waxed pine, massive and shining. Behind it, tilted back in a swivel chair, lounged a powerful figure, wearing a multi-coloured shirt, unbuttoned and open to the waist, and the dark mass of hair on his sunburned chest spread like wild vegetation. He was dark, sleek, and his face shone with a gloss derived from meticulous attention. There was nothing outstanding in his looks except that his nose was a little too broad and his blue eyes were hard. Gale noticed these things now, just as he'd noticed them on the first occasion of their meeting in New York several weeks earlier.

They were the sort of things you noticed about him no matter how many times one met him, he supposed. He saw that the other was holding an old book, as if he had been reading it. It looked an interesting sort of volume. He wasn't much of a reader, but he knew something about antique books. The man leaned forward and slapped the book on the desk so that it lay open, and Gale saw that it was an old, canvas-bound whaling logbook. This sort of stuff wasn't his cup of tea. He didn't know much about old American stuff, but he could glimpse the thumbnail silhouette of a whale which had been drawn on one thick, stained page.

The figure behind the desk looked up at him from beneath his dark eyebrows, and smiled. His teeth were white against the smooth, tanned face. His dentist had done a beautiful job on them.

'Hello, J.K.,' Gale said.

CHAPTER TWO

The man behind the desk didn't stir himself for Edwin Gale.
He just indicated him to pull up a chair. Accordingly, Gale took
the weight off his feet and leaned back in a big overstuffed armchair, and tried to look casual and relaxed. But the sweat made
his trouser legs stick to him at the back of his knees. J.K. looked
across the wide desk at him, and his voice was warm and deep,
but without any particular feeling.

'Swell to see you again.' There was a pause for a soft laugh.
'Glad you've had a profitable trip.'

'It's been all right,' Gale said stiffly.

'Sure, I know.' There was the soft laugh again. 'It's paid off.
What more can you ask from life?'

'I didn't anticipate coming right up here to collect.' He
allowed his tone to hold a peevish note.

'I'm sorry to give you the extra journey,' the other nodded
sympathetically. 'New York was kinda hot, and I just couldn't
content myself there, while my baby was sunning herself up
here.'

He stood up and threw a meaningful glance through the
french windows, towards the terrace below; he started to close
the windows. They closed noiselessly and the sounds from the
garden slid away. Instead of the humming of the bees and the
harsh cries of some seagulls out over Buzzard Bay, now the
room was heavy and silent and airless. The hammock was some
yards from the house, but J.K. was just the sort who took no
chances. He didn't even trust his baby.

Gale watched him, relaxed a little more in the chair. He noticed with some distaste the other's hairy legs that reached down from his perfectly tailored shorts like miniature tree trunks. He watched him while he padded across in blue canvas yachting shoes to an elaborate piece of furniture against one wall. It was built to look like a battered, sturdy old sideboard, and was adorned, as the sea chest had been, with paintings of spouting whales and mermaids, ship's wheels and anchors. He opened the doors to a television set, and cocktail cabinet complete with ice bucket. He took a silver shaker off the shelf above the ice bucket and a couple of exquisitely-cut glasses, filling them from the shaker. He handed one to Gale.

'Guessed you'd be thirsty.' He closed up the sideboard and took from the top two *pots de chambre*, decorated with roses and violets, one filled with cigarettes, the other with cheroots. 'Cigarette or cheroot?'

Gale took a cigarette. J.K. flicked a gold desk lighter and held the flame to the cigarette, lighting a cheroot for himself. He lit it, and after replacing the two receptacles back on the sideboard, he moved behind the desk once more.

'I was looking through this,' he said, pawing the volume he'd thrown on the desk when Gale had come in. 'Whaling logbook.' Gale nodded. He didn't show much interest, because that sort of stuff wasn't his cup of tea, and because he wanted to get down to business, collect, and beat it back to New York, and then take the plane for England, home and booty.

'Those were the days,' J.K. said. He obviously wasn't prepared to get down to business yet, and Gale twisted in his chair impatiently. He didn't like it. He could smell some funny caper in the heavy, silent air, and he didn't care for it.

'Buzzards Bay used to be thick with whales,' the other was saying. 'Until they wiped them out. I was reading about it, in some other book.' He stood up again, and his drink in his hand, crossed the floor, which mirrored him grotesquely in its dark, gleaming surface, and stood before the bookshelves. He took down an old volume and flipped through the thick, rough-edged pages as he came back to the desk. 'Listen to this. This is what happened when a bunch of small whales came in too near and were driven ashore. These small whales were called blackfish.'

He began reading in his warm, deep voice. It was as if, Gale thought, he was enjoying every word. 'When the school were discovered near the shore,' J.K. read, 'the fishermen getting outside of them in their dories, by halooing, sounding horns, and other noises, drove them, like frightened sheep, towards the beach. As soon as the hunters were in shoal water they left their boats, and jumped overboard, urging the silly fish on by outcries, splashing the water, and blows. Men, and even boys, waded boldly up to a fish, and led him ashore by a fin; or, if inclined to show fight, put their knives into him. They cuffed them, pricked them onward, filling the air with shouts, or with peals of laughter, as some pursuer, more eager than prudent, lost his footing, and became for the moment a fish. All this time the blackfish were nearing the shore, uttering sounds closely resembling groanings and lamentations. The calves kept close to the old ones. "Squealing," as one of the captors told me, "like young pigs." It was great sport, but not wholly free from danger, for the fish can strike a powerful blow with its flukes; and the air was filled with jets of water where they lashed it into foam.'

He put down the book on top of the whaling logbook, and looked at Gale with that soft laugh of his. Gale had been feeling a trifle sick to the stomach as he listened to the description of the slaughter, and the other's gloating tones did not help to allay his queasiness. He hoped now that the other had finished with horsing around before getting to the object of his visit, and a bitterness compounded of frustration and malevolence began to fill his heart. But he did not let it show on his face, there was no time for that. It only lurked at the back of his eyes. If J.K. saw what lay there, he gave no sign of it. Nor did he give any indication of wanting to bring Gale's visit to a close by talking about what he had come to Falmouth for.

'Yes,' he said, taking his cheroot from between his teeth and regarding its ash tip thoughtfully, 'the history of these parts is spattered with blood. When they weren't killing whales they were killing each other. Like Jennie Toppam, for instance.' He took a deep drag at his cheroot and lounged back in his chair expansively. Gale shifted uneasily in his own chair, uncrossed his legs, and crossed them again. J.K. was off on some more yattering. Gale's heart overflowed with malice. J.K. was doing this to him deliberately. Letting him sit there sweating on the top line, waiting to learn how he was to come out of the deal. Gale swore to himself he would never forgive J.K. for this.

'Out along Route 28,' the other was continuing, his smooth features urbane and his white teeth gleaming over the cheroot, 'at a little village called Cataumet, it was. This was a while back, but it made the headlines all over the States at the time. This Jennie Toppam was a foundling who became a nurse around these parts. Everybody said she was a wonderful nurse. Jolly Jennie she was known as. In 1901 during the summer she was nursing a Mrs. Alden Davis. On the 4th July Mrs. Davis died. Mrs. Davis's married daughter came from Chicago for the funeral. She took sick and she died, then Mr. Davis became ill and he died in Jennie's arms. Then the other daughter, Minnie, who was married to a sea captain named Gibbs, she died. "Plumb tuckered out," said Jennie, "the poor thing." The day of the funeral her husband put in from sea, to be told that his wife had just been buried. When he saw his wife's grave in the cemetery alongside the three others, Captain Gibbs fainted.'

For all that he was impatient for the other to get around to the business that had brought him to Falmouth, Gale found himself listening to J.K. He knew that the yarn-spinning was all part of J.K's idea to keep him in suspense, to make him feel on edge, so that he would be all that easier a pushover. He realized now that this was how J.K's mental processes worked. All the same, he found himself listening to this sordid story of long ago, he found himself hypnotized by those rich, warm, yet curiously matter-of-fact tones as he sat there in this silent, airless room, the sun bright outside, and the drink cool in his hand.

'Day after the funeral,' J.K. was saying, 'Jennie went out for a row in a little boat; she was wearing a silk dress with green stripes and a sailor hat with a green veil. While she was out rowing a local doctor named Wood called at the police station. "If you don't put that woman under arrest," he told them, "there'll be more deaths around here and another grave in the Davis lot. Go through her things while she's out and you'll find evidence to hold her." Because the doctor was so insistent the police searched her cottage, but Jennie came back in the middle of their search, and when she saw what was going on, she flew into a terrible rage. She was so mad she beat it out of Cataumet that very day.'

'But what the police found,' J.K. continued, 'was that an astonishing number of people had died when she was around. The bodies of the Davis family were exhumed. The autopsies took place in the carriage shed of the little church, where Jennie used to attend services every Sunday, and as a result she was picked up in New Hampshire, where she had gone to ground. She confessed everything. "Certainly I killed them," she said, "I been killing people for years." She began naming her victims, but after a while she stopped. "Thirty-one is all I can remember rightly, but that's no more than half. My memory," she explained, "ain't reliable. Mostly I used strychnine. Like to give 'em spasms. First I killed was Capt'n and Mrs. Toppam." They were the childless couple who had taken her out of the foundling home, given her their love and their name. The Cape Cod Borgia she was called, and the idea thrilled Jennie. "I killed for pleasure," she used to say; but she wasn't so happy when they found her insane and stuck her into a New Hampshire insane asylum. She was scared someone was going to poison her, and she wouldn't eat. So they had to put her in a straitjacket and forcibly feed her for years. All the same she lived to be eighty-one. "Miss Toppam never gave any trouble," the asylum superintendent said when she died. "She was a nice old lady and quiet as a mouse".'

The inside of Edwins Gale's mouth was warm as if it was full of blood. He swallowed with difficulty, but the sensation was still there. It always affected him like this, whenever he read of violence and sudden death, or saw it depicted in movies or on television, or heard of it, as he had been hearing now. This gruesome tale of murder and insensate evil in this quiet, easygoing part of the world where the gentle summer breezes came in from the warm sea, where the bees hummed and the flowers scented the air, and blossomed luxuriantly everywhere. J.K. was looking at him with that slow smile of amusement, as if he had been telling a smoking room story. Gale forced a smile and drew at his cigarette, hoping that the man behind the desk wouldn't notice that his hand was trembling slightly.

He wondered what J.K. would think if he could see into his mind then, as he held in it a mental picture of that Jennie whoever-she-was who had murdered for pleasure. He wondered what J.K. would think if he realized what twisted thoughts his little tale had sparked in his visitor's brain. The suppressed longing to know what it was like to kill, which at fleeting moments like these inexplicably flooded up from some dark abyss of his being.

Then it was gone; Gale's brain was clear again. He was sipping at his cool drink, his thoughts had clicked back into place, and he was calculating that surely J.K. had done with all the yattering, he must cut the cackle and get to the hosses.

It came then, quite calmly, without any change of expression in the other's smooth, sun-tanned features. He might have been continuing with Jennie Toppam's story; adding a coda to it. Instead he said: 'Now, just what were the terms we fixed?'

He jangled a key ring from his pocket and unlocked a drawer on a level with his well-massaged stomach. He took out several wads of dollar bills. They were hundred-dollar bills, Gale could see that. The white teeth chewed on the cheroot and a cloud of smoke drifted across the desk. J.K's eyes had narrowed a fraction as he looked at Gale through the blue haze, and without removing his gaze pushed across the notes to him. They slid crisply over the polished expanse of waxed pine. 'Five thousand dollars there. Count them for size. Which is your cut, okay?'

Gale was sweating again. This was it. This was the payoff. This was the fear that had been nagging at his guts ever since he knew he wasn't meeting J.K. in New York as originally arranged, that he had to fly to Cape Cod. This was the payoff that wasn't paying off so well. He stared at the wads of notes, that sickening stab hitting him in the stomach.

It was exactly half the money he was entitled to, exactly half what J.K. had agreed should be his cut.

CHAPTER THREE

Edwin Gale thought he might as well put up some pretence of a fight for his rights, even though he knew he was defeated already. Some instinct told him to mask his emotions, not to betray the seething hatred that brought the red mist swimming before his eyes. He had a momentary vision of the sea gulls he had watched earlier on, when he had stopped the car on his way to the house. He was recalling the sight of one of the birds wheeling up from the surface of the sea with a small, wriggling fish held in its beak. Right now, he thought, he was like that helpless fish.

'You agreed to take a twenty-five percent cut,' he said, keeping his tone light.

'Did I agree to that?' J.K's smooth dark eyebrows arched, and he moved his cheroot reflectively from one corner of his mouth to the other.

'You did.'

A glint of flinty amusement energized the corners of the other's jowls. 'You must have got it kind of wrong.'

The colour flared up into Gale's face and he leaned forward in his chair. Then he forced himself to relax again. 'That was the way I understood our arrangement,' he said.

J.K's expression was cool, calculating. His voice was patient, as if he was explaining something for the hundredth time. 'I guess I must have outlined the terms I operate on,' he said. 'A straight fifty-fifty basis. Nothing more or less.'

It was a bare-faced lie. Gale squirmed in silent fury at the cool effrontery of it. Still, he didn't let his face reflect his real feelings. J.K. had tricked him, as ever since the telephone call bringing him down from New York, he had vaguely suspected he would. He had pulled a fast one on him. And J.K. held all the winning cards. He supposed, he reflected ruefully, he should have caught on to it when J.K. fixed it that the old chump in Chicago was to pay the money not to him, but to the bald little man in Chicago who was J.K.'s stooge, and had been the go-between for the deal. But this was his first trip to America since the war. The angles were sharper now, the sharks devoured their own kind now.

'Seems like I have little choice,' he heard himself say at length. His voice was perfectly calm, there was a casual resigned shrug of the shoulders as he spoke. He fixed his thoughts on the knowledge that he would be on the plane for London that night. That was all that he wanted now. To get J.K. out of his sight. To get out of it, back to his own stamping ground, where he knew all the answers.

The other smiled his pleasure. 'You got to realize the service I provided. A stooge to steer you to the mug. My protection against any other party that might have muscled in on you. My own pet mouthpiece, the best lawyer in New York, to act for you, if things had gone wrong. I don't have to tell you those things cost money. All you had to do was to just meet the client and deliver the goods.' He leaned back and considered Gale benevolently. 'And,' he said, 'all expenses paid. Not bad for five grand.'

He took his cheroot from the corner of his mouth, put it back again, and he took a thick manilla envelope from a drawer and packed the notes in, sealing the flap, then he tossed the envelope across the desk. Gale slipped it into his inside pocket. It was stiff and the envelope creaked a little when he moved, but he didn't find it too uncomfortable. Without a word he got to his feet and stubbed out his cigarette into the ashtray on the corner of the desk. He didn't feel like finishing his drink.

'Sit down.' J.K. spoke quite pleasantly. 'It could be I got

something further to your advantage.'

Despite his impatience to be moving, on his way back to Hyannis and the plane for New York, Gale sat down again. Something in the other's tone made him curious, he did not know why. As things were to turn out in the long run, he shouldn't have stayed, he shouldn't have allowed his curiosity get the better of him. He should have gone. But he wasn't to know this, then.

'You got anything special lined up for when you get back to London?'

The airless room was suddenly warm, and Gale reached for his handkerchief. His curiosity grew as he mopped his moist face. He hadn't anything important to go back to, he would be taking it easy for a few weeks. Even with only five instead of ten grand he could afford to take things easy for a little.

'No,' he said thoughtfully. 'Nothing special in mind. But I've been in these parts long enough. I don't want to outstay my welcome.'

If the man at the desk noticed the sarcasm in Gale's voice he ignored it.

'This is a job in your own neck of the woods,' he said. He paused and looked at the long ash on his cheroot, whose aroma hung on the tobacco-smokey atmosphere. 'This could be right in your line.'

'Depends if it's on your easy terms.' Gale permitted himself a grin. He got a little satisfaction getting a crack back, but it left J.K. quite unruffled. His faint smile moved smoothly across his face. Then his white teeth held the cheroot again.

'I'll have no costs to cover,' he said. 'So I'll take just a flat ten percent for supplying the information, and the rest is yours.' He took a drink from the glass at his elbow. 'You can pay my cut to my contact in London. She'll want a cut herself, but you'll still stand to rake in enough to keep you sitting pretty for the rest of the year.'

'What are the snags?' Gale said.

'Snags? I can't see none. You could take it as smooth as an

elevator ride.'

Gale didn't let J.K. see more than a flicker of interest in his face as the other began talking incisively. But inwardly he was tense with the thrill of anticipation. It sounded from what J.K. was saying that this was something that could fit in very cosily with a scheme he had already tucked away in a pigeonhole at the back of his mind, against such an opportunity as was being outlined to him now. He was congratulating himself on his own foresight. He had felt it at the time, that one day he would be able to make something out of it to his own profit. His thoughts drifted back to London to focus on a mental picture of the dump in the King's Road, Chelsea.

'You listening?' J.K. said.

'I'm listening,' said Gale, watching J.K. thrust the cheroot stub into the ashtray.

'Guessed you would be.' He leaned hairy arms on the desk and clasped his hands. 'Here's how the situation looks to me. Now this chump named Lang is loaded, like I said. His family got oil in their blood and he inherited the results of their pioneering and labours. But his history needn't trouble you. All you'll want to know is that he's loaded, like I said before, and he's crazy about old books.' He paused and the white teeth gleamed. 'Provided they're genuine, natch.'

'Natch,' Gale said.

'He'll be in London about a week from now, if he sticks to his schedule. He's in Rome as of now. This is according to the dope I have on him. He passes through London on his way back to New York. So you have to—ah—interest him in a little some-thing in the time.' J.K. helped himself to another cheroot, and pushed the other *pot de chambre* across to Gale, who took a cigarette. The gold table lighter flamed. 'If it's any clue,' the other continued, 'he's spent a lot of time in Italy and Spain. Maybe he's a special interest there. You'll have to make your own assessment. But from where I'm sitting I'll say he's ripe for the right proposition.'

'Anybody's ripe for the right proposition at the right time,'

Gale said it mechanically. His mind was racing like a dynamo. His thoughts fastened themselves on the King's Road dump again. It couldn't fit in better if he had planned it himself, in anticipation of this opportunity turning up. He puffed coolly at his cigarette and kept the excitement out of his voice.

'I fancy I might be able to work out something,' he said.

'Don't sound so stuffed-shirt English,' the other man said. 'I tell you I'm giving you a break. You could clean up. Now listen. This Lang, he's the shy, retiring sort. He doesn't mix with high society. The gossip columnists don't go for him. He's nothing to look at and never does anything to attract attention. But Dolores knows him. She met him in Italy, she'll know when he arrives in London and the rest.'

'Dolores?'

'My contact in London,' J.K. said. He threw a glance over his shoulder in the direction of the hammock, and then leered at Gale as if he was taking him into his confidence about some guilty secret that possessed him. 'She's quite a baby. Contact her when you get back. Work out your own routine together. She'll collect my ten percent. What her take is, that'll be for you to fix with her. I'll be sending her my instructions.'

He sounded almost pompous, as if he was some top brass business executive handing out an assignment to an associate in a lower bracket. He wrote on a scribbling pad. 'Here's her private phone number.' He passed the slip of paper over and Gale glanced at it, then folded it and pushed it into his inside pocket along with the thick envelope.

J.K. sighed and leaned back lazily in his chair. 'I guess it's up to you now.' His eyes narrowed and there was a suggestion of a laugh in his voice. 'But you ain't going to do so badly out of meeting up with yours truly.'

'I'm grateful to you for the tipoff,' Gale smiled faintly, but didn't give his thoughts away. He hugged it to himself that the information that had been handed out to him opened up the possibility of a project after his own heart. A proposition which, if successfully handled, he told himself, if he couldn't handle it no one else could, should bring him a reward far in excess of anything he had achieved before. He would grasp the chance with both hands.

He might feel bitter at J.K. for the way he had treated him, but he could play this damned American at his own game now. He hated J.K's guts; but it wouldn't do to give that sentiment an airing now. He was a trickster. That was okay. He was a trickster himself; even if he hadn't cheated or double-crossed his pals. So far. But he'd every good reason to cheat J.K. out of his ten percent. That was justice.

He tapped the ash carefully from his cigarette into the ashtray, and returned the other's expectant look.

'I think it should work,' Edwin Gale said.

'It'll be like taking candy from a sleeping baby. And as soon as you get started, I'd like a report on the way it's shaping. I may have a trick or two you could add to your repertoire.'

'I'll keep you informed,' Gale said, with quiet confidence. He reached for his half-empty glass. His mind was cool and clear. He didn't notice J.K. go to the french windows and open them noiselessly, letting the breeze with its salty tang from off Buzzard Bay fill the big room, and letting in the humming of the bees and the grating cries of some of the gulls which had swooped over the garden beyond the terrace. He didn't hear J.K. call out endearments to the owner of the long, lovely legs in the hammock, or the soft, caressing reply. He was interested only in what he knew he was going to do. And he felt good about that.

He looked at his wristwatch. Sticking around while J.K. had yattered to him meant that he was cutting it fine if he was going to get the plane at Hyannis for New York. But he could make it. His gaze flickered at the french windows and the back in the multi-coloured shirt that was turned to him. What J.K. had spilled had been worth waiting to hear. A feeling of exhilaration uplifted him.

He glanced at his watch again and began to finish his drink.

CHAPTER FOUR

Gale was glad to be seeing New York once more. For one thing the city was cooler now, under the evening sky. For another thing, he was clear of J.K. and he had made Hyannis all right, and caught the plane. He had grabbed a quick lunch at Harbour Village in Hyannis before leaving on the return trip to New York.

As he had driven his hired car through the quiet villages and along the pleasant roads, with the blue inviting sea on one side, and the fields and shady woods on the other, he had wished he could have spent a few days in Cape Cod. The place possessed all the lazy distractions to entice the weary traveller, or the tired business man to relax in carefree comfort. But even if he had the time on his hands, he wouldn't have liked it, being so close to J.K. He had felt anxious to put as much distance as he could between himself and the man he had just left. That was how he had felt about J.K.

Now, back in New York, in the cab which was taking him from the airport to the Waldorf-Astoria, he patted his summer-weight jacket over the region of his pocket where the thick manilla envelope creaked with a gentleness that was almost affection. He stared blankly out of the taxi window. He didn't know where he was. He was bewildered by the teeming streets of Manhattan in daylight. He felt completely lost and had to rely on the cab driver. The traffic lights and intersections, the streets crowded with vehicles of all kinds and the crowds jostling the sidewalks; all formed a kaleidoscopic picture that confused him. Not that it bothered him. He let the driver do the worrying.

Now he saw that they had reached that part of the city where he was on familiar ground. The area of Park Avenue, 42nd Street, and 50th Street, the vicinity of the Waldorf-Astoria. Until then he hadn't been able to place himself at all, except in such obvious centres as Times Square and along Broadway. Now the cab was slowing to a stop outside the imposing entrance of the hotel. He paid off the cab and went into the cool, sumptuous hotel foyer.

He picked up his key and took the elevator, got out at his floor and went along the wide, soft-carpeted corridor and stopped outside his door. Inside the luxuriously-appointed room he locked the door and he picked up the telephone and ordered a large whisky and soda. Then he flopped into the comfortable chair and sighed with pleasure.

He always stayed at the best hotels. He liked luxury and he could often combine luxury with a little business. It was in the more exclusive and expensive places that he was able to rub shoulders with potential, wealthy chumps. To see him at ease in their own surroundings gave them confidence in him. His well-cut Savile Row clothes, his urbane good manners, suggested to those upon whom he wished to make the right impression that he was a man of substance.

That was why in London he paid such a high rent for his Park Lane flat and regarded it as a good investment. Like the frequent occasions when he lunched and dined at the Ritz or the Savoy, or Claridges and Brown's Hotel. He wondered where the man named Lang would choose to stay, when he came to London. He supposed the Dolores woman would have all the dope about that. He wondered what she was like. The name conjured up someone dark and exotic.

He was still musing pleasantly about the possibilities J.K. had opened up before his predatory mind, when the floor waiter brought his drink. He tipped the waiter generously, and locked the door as soon as he was alone again. He lit a cigarette and sipped his drink. Then he took out the thick manilla envelope and counted the contents through. It was all there. Five grand. About one thousand six hundred quid, in his language. And although he had been taken for a mug, tricked out of the amount due to him, so that he'd got only half he'd anticipated, his smile held no bitterness against J.K. now.

He calculated he was already on the way to avenging himself. He went into the bathroom and ran the bath, while he decided how he would spend the remaining hour or two that he had to kill in New York. He would be leaving Idlewild on the Stratocruiser. He had fixed his seat before flying down to Cape Cod. He was travelling light, there wasn't much packing for him to do. Sipping his drink, he sauntered across to the window and moved the edge of the curtain. He looked out in idle contemplation on the scene before him. The oncoming evening was beginning to pop with lights in the towering apartment blocks lining the avenue, while the street itself was thronged with vehicles and people. He recalled J.K's stooge in Chicago, the bald little loquacious middle-aged New Yorker who had aired his knowledge of New York's history. How three hundred years back a certain Captain Hudson in the employ of the Dutch West India Company had been the first white man to set foot in these parts when searching for a passage to India. Later had come the Dutch traders to barter with the Indians for animal skins and furs; then a few years after the first Dutch settlement was established the Dutch West India Company bought Manhattan Island for twenty-four dollars' worth of hunting knives. Then fifty years later, an English fleet had sailed in and taken over, and named the place New York after the Duke of York, the brother of King Charles II.

It occurred to him that it wouldn't do any harm for him to mug up a bit on the discovery of America and the historical stuff that went with it; in view of the scheme that was building up at the back of his mind, it would be a useful sort of patter to be able to come out with when the occasion called for it.

Looking down towards Park Avenue now, it was difficult to credit that this which was now Manhattan had once been no more than a few hutments and shacks and wigwams. It was a pity, he thought, he hadn't had the time to look around more. He would have liked to have browsed in the bookshops and museums, toured the Rockefeller Centre, appreciated the view from the Empire State Building and toured the island by boat just to see if the Manhattan skyline did live up to the view from a cinema seat.

He let the curtains fall back into place and finished his drink, and went into the bathroom and lowered himself into the sunken bath. Luxuriating in the warm water, and lathering himself with aromatic soap he let his thoughts drift back to the house at Falmouth and the slim, sun-tanned legs of the girl in the gently-swinging hammock. J.K's baby. He tried to imagine what she looked like. Young and blonde, he decided, pretty and wide-eyed perhaps.

He relaxed and drifted off into a reverie which was dominated by a slim, blonde pretty girl with long suntanned legs. She would be his baby. Only in the past it hadn't worked out like that. Somehow, that was something he hadn't gone in for. He'd been too busy cooking up schemes to give much time to women. And now he was pushing forty-five, and although the idea of a pretty blonde appealed to him, the prospect of having to chase one up bored him. He remembered someone saying that the older a man got, the less attractive he was to women while the more choosey he became. Perhaps this Dolores might turn out to be someone he could go for and who would go for him.

Presently he was putting on a fresh silk shirt with its monogram neatly embroidered on it over his heart. He knotted a dark, silk-knitted tie under his plump chin, and began getting into the dark grey worsted suit. He pushed a fine white lawn handkerchief into his breast pocket, while he decided he would have dinner up in the Starlight Roof restaurant atop of the hotel, and then make tracks for Idlewild.

He regarded his reflection in the long mirror for a few moments, and satisfied with what he saw, turned to the lightweight suit he had discarded. He transferred the precious manila envelope from it, folding it back a couple of inches down one side and fitting it carefully in the inside pocket of his grey suit, so that it lay flat without bulging. It felt quite comfortable, the occasional creak which made its presence felt filled him with a sense of well-being. He folded his clothes carefully and packed them into their suitcase, and then lighting a cigarette he went out of the room.

A feeling of deep satisfaction filled him. Despite the shabby treatment he had suffered at the hands of J.K., he had forgotten the paroxysm of silent fury that had obscured his vision with a murderously-red haze. J.K. had cracked the whip and he had obeyed. But that was done with. Another transaction had been completed and he had come out of it with a nice profit; he had come out of it in the clear, there'd been no trouble at all.

And now another project was opening up, a deal that promised a really big killing, and this time it would not be J.K. who held the whip hand.

He glanced at his wristwatch, regarded himself in the mirror once more for a moment, and gave his handkerchief a touch, then went out of the room. He locked the door, slipping the key into his pocket and made his way towards the elevators. He suddenly realized he was feeling quite hungry, and he began turning over in his mind what he would like to eat. Steak Diane, he thought, with some iced melon to precede it; he would have salad with the steak, and just a few *sautéed* potatoes. He ought to watch his weight a bit, he supposed. There had been a bit of a bulge there, which even the cunning of his tailor hadn't quite streamlined away. He thought he might use half a bottle of Vin Rosé to go with the Steak Diane.

He pressed the button to call the elevator and noted the illuminated indicator which told him it was on its way. In a moment or two the ornate elevator doors opened with a sibilant purr and he made to step into the luxurious interior. As he did so, however, a figure stepped out. Gale glanced up at the lean features from which a pair of dark eyes flickered over him.

There was complete disinterest in their expression, but at the same time Gale experienced the uncomfortable sensation that those eyes were penetrating into the innermost recesses of his mind.

Instinctively, as if faced with a sudden unexpected danger, he put his hand up over the pocket wherein reposed the manila envelope, while he stood aside to allow the tall, angular figure to pass. He glimpsed the dark hair above the hawk-like face, the temples streaked with grey. Something about the man struck a distant chord in his memory. He felt sure he had seen those sharply-chiselled saturnine features before. Perhaps it was his photograph in a magazine or newspaper. Some politician or similarly eminent public personality; no, that wasn't the sort with which Gale associated him. Something quite different, unusual. But for the life of him he couldn't place him. There was a remoteness, a forbidding, almost sinister, quality that the figure exuded.

The dark gaze flickered past him and Gale could not resist turning to watch the tall, purposeful form move off with raking strides. Idly he noted the dark suit of unmistakably English cut. Something about his appearance convinced him that the man wasn't an American.

Inexplicably Gale experienced a tremor pass through him. Some sensation at the soles of his feet, as if the hotel had recoiled slightly to the impact of a minor earthquake. Then the feeling had gone, he blinked his eyes, his aplomb returned as he got into the elevator and pressed a finger on a button.

The doors slithered shut, and scowling faintly to himself as he racked his brains in an effort to recall who it was that he had just encountered, the elevator bore him up to the Starlight Roof restaurant, high above New York.

CHAPTER FIVE

Gale had decided not to use the airport bus, but to leave earlier in a cab, with the object of obtaining a farewell look at Manhattan and Brooklyn on his way to Idlewild. After an enjoyable, relaxed meal, where everything had been to perfection—the cooking, the service, the sumptuousness of his surroundings in the elegant restaurant—he had returned to his room. A choice Havana cigar was stuck in his face, which was a trifle red now from the effects of the excellent Vin Rosé, and he had packed his last-minute requisites and then rode down in the elevator and settled his account.

Now, with a sense of elation and anticipation at the prospect of the trip, he leaned back in the cab. In his brief stay he had seen little enough of New York, and it seemed a pity he was forced to take his leave without even having gained a tourist's impression of the place. So going out to Idlewild this way would be some compensation. He had instructed the driver to take him along the most picturesque route commensurate with the time available.

They had moved off from the Waldorf-Astoria out into the traffic stream down towards Grand Central Terminal, across 42nd and along Fourth Avenue. Turning right into East 23rd, they went past Madison Square and into Fifth Avenue, Gale obtaining a glimpse of the Washington Arch as they ran beneath it. At Washington Square they turned left and then right again into Broadway as far as Canal Street.

The cabby continued via the Bowery, skirting Chinatown, to

reach the municipal buildings in Park Row, where they turned for Brooklyn Bridge. Crossing the bridge the driver decided to impress his passenger with a sudden flow of statistics. Six thousand and sixteen feet long the bridge was, he said, its centre span a hundred thirty-three feet above the East River, and although it was opened in 1883, it was still one of the most beautiful bridges New York had to offer. Gale sounded suitably impressed.

The cabby lapsed into silence, having apparently exhausted his store of information, and in Brooklyn they passed close to the U.S. Navy Yard. The car was heading in an easterly direction. Gale would have liked to have gone south and taken a look at fabulous Coney Island, but there was no time to make a detour of that distance. He'd have to be content with a glimpse of the crowded, multicoloured scene from the plane. Through Brooklyn and Queens they went, and then they were at the airport, all bustle and movement and brightly lit in the evening shadows.

In the reception block he went through the customs, and when the formalities were over he bought the evening papers and some glossy magazines. He sat in the lounge and waited for his flight to be called. An assortment of passengers waited with him. He buried his attention in a magazine until at length his flight was called over the loudspeakers, and he joined the rest of the passengers to troop up the stairway into the hull of the Stratocruiser. As the engines fired off one after another, Gale sat himself down in one of the adjustable reclining chairs next to a window.

He was occupied with the preliminaries of fastening his safety belt, while the engines were revved to full throttle, as someone sat next to him. He threw a glance at his fellow passenger. It was the solitary occupant of the elevator at the Waldorf-Astoria which he had called to take him up to the Starlight Room. The tall, dark brooding figure who Gale had thought was strangely familiar. Came the sudden jerk as the brakes were released and the aircraft moved forward towards the runway. At the instant—it may have been the shock of suddenly finding him sitting quietly beside him—Gale knew who he was. He knew where he'd seen his photograph: it had been in the newspapers at home, and there had been pictures and stories in the American newspapers during the past few days.

Just for a fraction of a second Gale wondered if there was more to it than mere coincidence in the fact that the tall, saturnine-faced man should have been staying at the same hotel, and now travelling in the same plane with him. Then he dismissed the suspicion as being ridiculous. There could be no possible reason why he should entertain a moment's misgiving or feel the slightest hint of fear from that quarter. Reassured, he smiled to himself. This might turn out to be quite amusing.

There would be ample opportunity now for him to make the acquaintance of the man next to him. What more natural than that they should get into conversation when they were to be travelling companions until the next morning? But he must take his time and choose his moment. He didn't know whether he had in turn been recognized as a result of the fleeting encounter at the hotel elevator. The tall, angular man hardly gave the impression of being the easily approachable type. No sense, Gale decided, in risking his resentment by being too obvious about scraping an acquaintance with him.

He didn't even glance at his companion again. He looked out of the window at the runway falling away below them. They climbed up over the sea, grey now in the failing light, and made a wide turn northeastward towards Nova Scotia, and already the spread of land and water below them was resembling a map. Here and there in some inlet Gale could discern the glint of ships' lights twinkling up at him as if winking a last farewell.

The great aircraft climbed higher, and soon he was looking down on what he guessed must be the sprawling arc of Boston, and he made out the crooked finger of Cape Cod, but he couldn't pick out the town of Falmouth. He suddenly wondered how J.K. and his baby were spending their time down there. He had a mental picture of those very white teeth bared at him across the wide desk, and he was recalling the heavy, airless silence of the room. Soon the shoreline receded, and they seemed to be curiously alone high over the fast-darkening wastes of the Atlantic Ocean.

Gale closed his eyes and relaxed comfortably and stretched out his legs. He glanced idly at the dark, attractive head of the girl in front of him. She had lowered the back of her reclining seat and already appeared to be asleep with her safety belt still fastened around her waist. Maybe she was a bad traveller and hoped to lose herself and her surroundings before they had any adverse effect on her stomach or her mind.

Gale felt sure it was all psychological. The knowledge of being suspended in the air in a metal cylinder, with no other means of support than engines and controls which depended on oil and electricity and on humans who seemed frail and puny in the vast emptiness of the sky. That, more than anything, Gale thought, was the kind of mental aberration that made your stomach queasy. Not the ride or the sensation of flying, because when you kept your attention on your immediate surroundings, the agreeably furnished pressurized cabin, there was no sensation of flying. It was as smooth as sitting in a favourite armchair at home.

The direction of his thoughts recalled the man next to him. What he'd read about him in a Chicago or a New York newspaper, and which hadn't gripped his attention at the time, was to do with a conference he'd come from London to attend. To do with some psychological stuff or something like that, or maybe it was to do with sociology. Or was it criminology? Maybe it was that. Maybe it was all three. Then his mind went back to his photos and the references to him in the London newspapers. Some strange business at a Soho nightspot. The Black Moth, that was the name of the dump. Gale had been there once or twice, though he'd never met the boss who'd gone and got himself rubbed out by his jealous wife, or whatever she was.

From the corner of his eye he could see that the chiselled aquiline features were bent upon what appeared to be a scientific journal. Gale wondered what line he should take to make his first approach. And then a man passed along the aisle and disappeared down the stairway just aft of the passenger entrance. Gale realized he was going to the bar lounge on the lower deck.

He stirred himself ostentatiously, rising slowly and turning towards his companion, who glanced up at him. Once again Gale experienced the sensation that those dark eyes were capable of probing deep into his mind. 'Forgive me,' he said, moving out into the aisle. 'But if we're going to spend the night half-sitting, half-reclining, I think it calls for a little exercise now.' He stopped and said with well-simulated surprise: 'But I've seen you before.'

'Indeed?'

'Now where the devil—? I know, you were getting out of the elevator and I was getting in. At the Waldorf-Astoria this evening.'

'I have been staying there; but forgive me if I don't recall the incident you mention.'

For some reason, though he couldn't put his finger on it, Gale had the impression that the man was lying. And once more it occurred to him that there was more than mere coincidence to their two encounters. But he brushed the suspicion aside again as being utterly uncalled for. He played it carefully now, not sounding too effusive or too eager to make anything of it.

'And though I couldn't fix it at the time,' he said. 'I knew you were someone well known.'

'I'm sure you flatter me unduly.'

'It's just come to me now,' Gale said, 'you're the famous Dr. Morelle.'

The dark glance that flickered over him was enigmatic, as was the faint smile that shadowed the corners of the firm mouth. The expression might have been one indicative of displeasure or annoyance. Those narrowed eyes, hooded now in a manner reminiscent, Gale thought, of some bird of prey, might be concealing a certain vainglorious smugness at the knowledge that their owner was the object of public interest. The broad lofty brow was bent in reluctant acknowledgment of Gale's recognition.

'I am Dr. Morelle.' The tone was suave, the words were uttered in a tone of suitable condescension, as if Dr. Morelle was somewhat unwilling to admit his identity to a complete stranger.

'I'm very honoured that I'm travelling in your company,' Gale said. 'I've read a lot about you, of course, and to meet you like this, it's really thrilling.'

Dr. Morelle made a deprecating murmur.

'And talking about that exercise,' Gale said. 'I didn't mean any more than stretching the legs as far as the bar. Would you care to join me in a snifter?'

Dr. Morelle's gaze was levelled on him again, and for a moment Gale imagined he detected in it a glint of amusement, and he wondered what could be the reason for it. Had he over-done it, despite his resolution to play it gently? He couldn't see how. Perhaps he had sounded a bit too ingenuous, and it didn't go with his appearance and manner. There was nothing of the tourist about him, he knew. He shrugged mentally. He had over-acted it: so what if he had? It didn't amount to a row of beans if he failed to strike an acquaintanceship with this Dr. Morelle.

And then it flashed through his mind that he didn't know what had prompted him to try it on, anyway. The man could do him no good. In fact, come to think, it might be the other way, it wasn't outside the bounds of possibility that he could be in a position to cause him a bit of trouble. He was friendly with the police, after all.

What then had sparked his wish to get pally with this strange, aloof figure whom he had encountered quite by chance? Some kind of bravado, he told himself. Like whistling in the dark. Some twist to his subconscious which made him want to get to know someone better who was on the other side of the fence. Like saying good night to a passing cop. Or perhaps it was because there lurked at the back of his mind still that faint suspicion that there was more to it than chance that the two of them should have been in the same hotel together at the same time, and now they were sitting together high above the Atlantic on the same plane.

'You're very kind,' Dr. Morelle said smoothly. 'I think I should like a drink.'

CHAPTER SIX

Gale could not help feeling a certain smug amusement as a result of his fortuitous encounter with Dr. Morelle. He congratulated himself at the manner with which his eminent fellow passenger had responded to his preliminaries at scraping acquaintanceship with him. They had exchanged with each other general impressions about New York and the United States over a drink in the small but luxurious, softly-lit lounge bar on the lower deck of the great, gently pulsating aircraft, while the night engulfed the sky and sea below.

Just before Gander they had returned upstairs to their seats. There had come the familiar instructions: 'Fasten your safety belts, please,' and the plane was circling over the airport, their first and last stop before Europe. 'We'll be down any moment,' Gale said conversationally. Dr. Morelle nodded. 'Marvellous how you take it all for granted,' Gale said. 'Just as if you were catching a train.'

A brief halt at Gander, and they were speeding through the starlit sky once more, high over the unseen Atlantic, on the great hop of their journey that was to bring them by early breakfast-time to Prestwick, and arrival at London Airport in time for mid-morning coffee.

As he relaxed in his comfortable chair, enjoying a Le Sphinx cigarette which Dr. Morelle had offered him from his thin, gold cigarette case, Gale was thinking that though he had built up his own character and background for the benefit of the man who sat quietly beside him, he had not found him at all communicative. Dr. Morelle had listened politely, attentively perhaps, but he had contributed nothing to the conversation concerning either his past or present activities. Gale had attempted subtly to glean from him some knowledge of the part he played in those famous criminal cases with which he recalled Dr. Morelle having been associated. But all he had learned was how much Dr. Morelle had enjoyed his lecture tour of the States, how he had met eminent American medical men, criminologists, and sociologists, and how he had discussed with them many interesting problems.

Dr. Morelle had made only the most guarded references to his meetings with the police chiefs in California and Chicago; he had barely touched upon his visits to the police bureaus of San Francisco and New York. Whatever Gale had consciously hoped to gain out of it, this encounter at any rate paid off little. He supposed, he had been prompted, that he would acquire some knowledge of Dr. Morelle's mental processes, how a brilliant mind, such as it was, worked; what made the man tick. But for all his gently persistent questions, plus an exaggerated display of interest on his part, Gale had to admit that he had quite failed to size up his fellow passenger. He was able to elicit observations and comments in a general way, but at no time could he feel that he would ever know what went on behind those finely-chiselled features, that saturnine expression. And Gale was not so much interested in the people in general or their problems, sociological or philosophical, as he was in Dr. Morelle himself.

He glanced round him. Many of the passengers had switched off their reading lights and had adjusted the backs of their seats to a reclining position, preparatory to settling down for the night. Gale wondered whether Dr. Morelle might be about to do the same, and he turned to him at the same moment as he pressed the button of the service bell. He exhaled a cloud of smoke and smiled.

'Don't know about you,' he said. 'But I don't feel so sleepy as I should. I could use a nightcap. Will you have something?'

Dr. Morelle shook his head. The neatly-uniformed hostess

appeared. She took Gale's order, and then glanced at Dr. Morelle. She was a pretty brunette and Gale saw the admiring look in her eyes. She was obviously impressed by the angular figure with the domed, intellectual head. 'Nothing for you, Dr. Morelle?' she said, and Gale realized she had recognized him. Dr. Morelle made a negative murmur and the hostess, flashing him a brilliant smile, disappeared towards the pantry at the tail end of the aircraft, returning shortly with a tray containing a large whisky and a soda siphon. Gale squirted the soda into his glass. As he sipped his drink, Dr. Morelle lit a cigarette.

'I can't help envying you your work,' Gale said, deciding to try another conversational gambit. 'Though I suppose as a psychiatrist you would regard envy as not the sort of emotion I ought to possess?' He chuckled over the rim of his glass.

Dr. Morelle regarded the tip of his Le Sphinx for a moment. 'There are other emotions which might be regarded as potentially more destructive,' he said.

Gale nodded sagely. 'That's what I mean,' he said. 'What could be more interesting than observing the why and wherefore of men's minds. To look into a man's innermost thoughts. To study human nature. That's a real job of work now. Not like my business, which is as fusty and musty as they come.' He paused, and Dr. Morelle's glance flickered over him.

'You mean you are an author?'

'I haven't the creative mind,' Gale said, allowing a wistful smile to play over his mouth. 'No, I make my living out of what they write. I deal in books. First editions, manuscripts, that sort of thing. The more antique the better.'

'It would appear to offer you opportunities to travel,' Dr. Morelle said.

'I'm not the stay-at-home type,' Gale said. 'My business does get me around, and I'm grateful for that.'

'That would be regarded by some as possessing certain compensations.'

Gale chuckled again, nodding in agreement. 'I suppose I could count my blessings,' he said.

'You specialize in any particular type of literature?' Dr. Morelle said, showing some slight interest, Gale decided.

'Not particularly,' he said smoothly. 'I just keep an eye open for important items which come my way. Like this trip I've just made to Chicago. I had a buyer there who is crazy about anything to do with Leonardo da Vinci.' He thought he detected a quizzical glint in Dr. Morelle's glance. 'I'd managed,' he went on, 'to obtain a rare volume of one of his notebooks, came across it in Paris.'

He broke off. Dr. Morelle's glance had become abstracted. 'Leonardo, eh?' he mused. 'You will have seen his "Last Supper" in the convent church of Saint Maria delle Grazie?'

'Matter of fact, I haven't. My travels never got me to Florence.'

'It wouldn't have mattered if they had,' Dr. Morelle said. 'The church of Saint Maria delle Grazie happens to be in Milan.'

'I mean Milan,' Gale said. 'Of course.' He covered up his confusion by taking a sip from his glass. He would have to watch his step here. He mugged up a hell of a lot about da Vinci in order to help him put it over to that chump in Chicago. But Dr. Morelle sounded as if he might be a bit ahead of him. He was the erudite type all right, he scowled to himself momentarily. He was wondering what had made him start yattering about it. He tried to think of something to say which would switch the conversation.

'One of those many-sided men of pure genius that the world produces only once or twice in the course of centuries,' Gale heard Dr. Morelle saying. 'He did more than paint. He invented paints and worked out a whole philosophy of painting.'

'I know.' Gale nodded trying to sound as if he did know. He started calling on his memory to revive the facts and information he had amassed in order to make a suitable impression during his Chicago trip.

'He thought out flying machines,' he said. 'Tanks, drainage systems, an incredible variety of things. Went off with Caesar Borgia as a sort of engineer, planning canals and harbours, and so forth. His notebooks are among the most astonishing documents in the history of mankind.' He was gratified to note Dr. Morelle's reflective expression, and he continued confidently: 'You can see in these notebooks of his how he studied and collected types of mankind.' He smiled. 'Almost in your line of business, wasn't he?'

Dr. Morelle gave a deprecatory shrug. 'He can be said to have graduated from a most minute study of insects and reptiles to objects of terrifying loathsomeness.' For a moment Gale fancied those dark eyes were boring into him with that peculiar intensity which was almost mesmeric in its power. He ran his tongue over his lips and reached again for his drink.

'Certainly,' Dr. Morelle said, returning to what was in his mind, 'the figures in his "Last Supper" were all taken from existing types of humanity.' He paused and sighed. 'That masterpiece which will cease all too soon to exist. Painted as it is on plaster which is slowly crumbling away.'

'Isn't there some strange yarn told about the picture?' Gale said.

Dr. Morelle was observing him once more. 'Do you mean,' he said, 'the story of how he found the model of his figure of Judas Iscariot?'

Gale nodded, and infused his tone with as much enthusiasm as he could. He had heard the yarn from his Chicago victim, and it had quite given him the creeps then. Somehow he had felt it was a sort of bad omen, and he didn't want to hear it again. Then he realized that he himself had brought up the subject into the conversation, and he frowned to himself. This character Dr. Morelle was having a bit of an odd effect on him.

'He needed to find models for Christ and the Apostles,' Dr. Morelle was saying. 'By good fortune, he found an amazingly handsome young man with a shining personality who was ideal for the Christ figure, and into his portrayal he devoted much loving care.' He paused dramatically. 'He never hurried, but worked with care and integrity quite unsurpassed by any painter. Years passed. He found his models for Peter, John, and the rest of the disciples. All except Judas, the model for whom he could not find. He visualized a man who would look the very arche-type of villainy and treachery. He searched the vilest gaols, but not one could yield as evil a man as the Judas whom Leonardo had created in his imagination and waited now to express with his brush. And then, at last,' Dr. Morelle said, 'he found his model. In a condemned cell in a small Italian gaol, a double-dyed assassin under sentence of death. Leonardo visited him in his cell with his notebooks, sketching him and committing to his pages every lineament of degradation in those depraved features, every shift and movement of that murderous figure. And so he painted his profound conception of Judas Iscariot into the "Last Supper". He talked to the vicious creature who was his model as he sketched him. The condemned man sneered at him. "Once before," he said, "an artist painted me. I don't know what you want with my portrait, but I can tell you that this other painted me as Our Lord".'

Edwin Gale shot a quick look at Dr. Morelle. 'You don't mean—?' he started to say, then broke off.

'"What was your name then?" Leonardo asked the man,' Dr. Morelle was continuing. '"Isola," the man said. "I have been called many names since. But that was what it was then." There was silence. Then Leonardo said: "God have mercy on your soul, unhappy man. You are the same that I depicted as the Son of God." In the twenty years which had passed, while Leonardo had been working on his great picture, the young man who had been his model for Christ had sunk from all that was noble to all that was vile.'

Dr. Morelle turned to gaze thoughtfully out of the window at the passing darkness, which reflected the glow of the exhaust of the great engines which bore the aircraft through the night. Gale finished his drink and eyed the gaunt profile beside him. 'It's quite a story,' he said. 'And I suppose it's got a kind of moral to it, wouldn't you say?'

The hawk-like face turned back to him, a thin smile curving the corners of the mouth. 'There is a moral to it, without a doubt. Which is, don't believe everything you hear. No, enthralling as it is, I'm afraid the story is apocryphal. One of those legends which has become associated with his name, but which has never been substantiated. Similarly, tales have grown up about his other famous pictures, the "Mona Lisa", whose enigmatic smile is popularly supposed to mask the tormented soul of the woman whom Leonardo took as his model. The truth is that she was the wife of a personal friend of his named del Gioconda. Leonardo took four years to complete the portrait, and in order to prevent Lisa del Gioconda from looking bored and losing her smile which he found so mysteriously appealing, he used to tell her amusing stories, and play little jokes.'

Gale smiled amusedly. Then he said, with mock ruefulness: 'And I'm supposed to be an expert. Next time I want to learn the inside dope on this sort of stuff, I'll know who to come to.'

Dr. Morelle made no response. Gale tried to imagine what was going on behind that bland expression, but it was as impossible, he thought, to penetrate as that enigmatic smile on the blessed "Mona Lisa" picture Dr. Morelle had been talking about. 'Anyway,' he said lightly, 'I hope you'll bear me in mind if ever you hear of anyone having a rare book they want to sell. Or buy.' He was smiling, but he knew it sounded forced and he picked up his glass, saw that it was empty, and replaced it.

Gale glanced out of the window. He could see nothing below, a black void separated them from the unseen ocean thousands of feet down there. But the velvet dome of the sky was pinpointed with a myriad of stars that glittered coldly and remote. He adjusted his seat to a semi-reclining position and turned out the reading light.

'It's been very enjoyable, Doctor,' he said. The nightcap was beginning to take effect, and he stifled a yawn. 'I hope you will sleep well.'

'Good night,' Dr. Morelle said softly.

Soon Dr. Morelle could hear the deep, regular breathing of the sleeping figure beside him. He himself remained wide awake, his head back, his gaze narrowed, fixed upon the shadowed ceiling, his mind speculative.

Presently Dr. Morelle's ruminations were filled with a familiar, softly-rounded face, whose large grey eyes were wide behind horn-rimmed spectacles. While he had been away she would have been kept busy enough at 221b Harley Street. That was one of her many good qualities, he told himself. He could rely on her to be as efficient and conscientious during his absence as she was when he was there. He experienced a feeling of warmth towards that slim little figure who occupied his mind's eye. It would be pleasant to be back, he thought. A smile that was not without a certain smugness flitted over his shadowed features.

Then suddenly a frown drew those dark, somewhat Mephistophelian eyebrows together. Had she received that last-minute cable? He had decided to change his departure date from New York, leaving a day earlier, and had sent off that morning his new time of arrival at London Airport. Had she, he wondered, received the cable? His eyes closed and drowsily; he pondered whether or not he had made it clear that he expected to be met with a hired car. There swam across the screen of his imagination a vision of Miss Frayle's fluttery, excitable reaction when she realized that he would be back a day sooner than she expected him. Would she be with the car to meet him at the airport?

The man who had introduced himself to him as Edwin Gale stirred beside him, and Dr. Morelle opened one eye to glance incuriously at the too-smooth flesh over the cheekbones, the mouth sagging a little open above the weakish chin. Then the deep regular breathing was resumed. Dr. Morelle closed his eye and slowly turned his head. In a few moments he too fell asleep.

The Stratocruiser pushed onwards like some remorseless bird, and Dr. Morelle's dreams became invaded by a man whom he knew in his dream to be Leonardo da Vinci, though at the same time it was himself. And he was sketching a manacled, terrifying creature in a dark, doom-laden condemned cell. A creature whose face was not that of Judas Iscariot, it was Edwin Gale's.

CHAPTER SEVEN

They would be down in ten minutes' time.

The passengers had begun to stretch themselves, and to collect their books and magazines, handbags, and hand luggage. The dark-haired girl in front of Edwin Gale looked out of the window, where the sky was a brilliant blue, cloudless and bright with sunlight, and then she turned her head to smile, for no particular reason that Gale could think of, at Dr. Morelle, who had just lit an after-breakfast Le Sphinx.

Most of the other passengers were glancing expectantly out of the windows; while the air hostesses, trim and bright-eyed and cheerfully friendly, were moving to and fro, busy attending to last-minute orders of tea or coffee.

Gale smiled cynically to himself at the atmosphere that was generated by the attitude of excitement and anticipation about him, as if most of those aboard regarded the Stratocruiser as the only aircraft in the sky bearing them like an eager dart straight to its target, London Airport. He knew from experience that it might be half an hour or more before they actually got down onto the deck.

In the cockpit the pilot and his copilot sat before their instrument panel and were now under the supervision of Approach Control. Coming in from Epsom, the plane had taken its place in the continuously moving queue of other incoming air traffic, and like these others, it would begin the final approach to the runway.

In the darkened room on the seventh floor of the airport

control tower, the Stratocruiser was caught on the picture of one of the controllers' screen. The pilot had radioed the plane's flight and estimated time of arrival, and the tickertape messages were chattering out of the machines, to be duly circulated to the departments concerned. He was now about eight miles from the deck and the pilot said he was coming in.

Led towards the first line of approach by Number 1 Radar Director, kept supplied with weather information, he was told the runway he was to use. Visibility was okay, so he didn't have to worry about the I.L.S. dial on the instrument panel. Now Number 1 had handed him over to Number 2 Radar Director up there in the control tower. The pilot was getting his final course adjustments so that he could put his ship in a position to begin its approach to the runway. His attention was upon the electronic instrument before him. Soon he would be able to get his visual guidance to the runway threshold.

There it was, now he could see the runway, and he was radioing Number 2 accordingly. Number 2 handed him over to the Ground Control sitting at his raised desk high up in the glass cupola at the zenith of the control tower.

Down there the airport was a six-pointed star of runways, with the gleam of windows from the sprawling buildings and the glint of planes in the sunlight.

Behind the cockpit, the passengers were talking animatedly, now they were aware that their journey really was almost over, and the excitement which had abated a little while the plane circled the airport was rising again. Expectancy gleamed even more brightly upon most faces. Gale turned to Dr. Morelle. 'We'll be down in a minute,' he said. And Dr. Morelle nodded through a cloud of cigarette smoke.

Gale was regarding him with a fresh slant. This was the nasty moment coming up. This was where, experienced and assured air traveller that he was, he always experienced that ghastly fear. This was it, when the plane was about to touch down, that the palms of his hands inevitably ran with sweat. He had to reach for his crisp white handkerchief to dry them. Some people, he knew, felt the same way at the moment of the takeoff as well; but with him that part was no worry at all, it was the coming in to land, only that.

He caught Dr. Morelle's look, intent upon him. He forced a grin to his stiff lips. He wondered if it affected Dr. Morelle in any way. Did his hands drip with sweat, or did he feel sick to the stomach at the takeoff or touchdown, or both? For all those saturnine features told him, he was thinking now, as the aircraft tilted in its circling flight, Dr. Morelle might be about to step from any first-class railway carriage onto the station platform. He noticed the Le Sphinx as Dr. Morelle held it for a moment to tap off the ash. The strong-looking fingers couldn't have been any steadier.

'Fasten your safety belts, please,' came the cool, friendly voice of the pretty brunette air hostess. Tension suddenly gripped the aircraft.

While up there in the cockpit, the pilot, the copilot beside him, sat relaxed, the glassy nose of the ship pointed down towards the hundred yards' wide runway, directly ahead, running on for a mile and three-quarters. Now it was all his, and as easily as if he was parking a car alongside a pavement kerb, the wheels touched down, with an almost imperceptible bump.

They were on the deck, gliding over the runway, slowing gently to a halt. From the glass cupola, where he had a panoramic view of the entire airport, the Ground Control was guiding the pilot through the mesh of taxiways. It stopped on the apron before one of the ramps that led up to the covered way to the passengers' gallery. The roar of its engines died away.

They were home and dry.

Edwin Gale stood aside in the aisle of the plane and flashed on his charming smile, indicating to Dr. Morelle to precede him. With a little knot of passengers they went down the short flight of stairs at the exit door and stood together on the tarmac. All about them the hot sunlit air reverberated with the sounds of aircraft engines. The open throttle of a plane about to take off; the roar of an aircraft taxiing into position; the rhythmic throb of aircraft in the sky above.

Gale followed Dr. Morelle onto the ramp and into the quietness of the airside gallery, with its wood-wool, sound-absorbing ceiling. Now they were walking past the windows which were decorated with tropical flowers, their scent sweet on the warm atmosphere. They were in the low-roofed hall where the Customs officers were awaiting them. Their luggage which had been sent up by conveyer belt was already there.

Gale was still close to Dr. Morelle as they went through the Customs. He caught the friendly, respectful smile that the uniformed official attending him gave Dr. Morelle. 'Good morning, Dr. Morelle. Hope you had a pleasant trip?'

'Most agreeable, thank you.'

Now all the formalities were over, passports and other documents checked, and the passengers were straying out through the doors into the Main Concourse. Here against the background of the huge windows stretching from the marble floor to the lofty ceiling which overlooked the runways was the bustle of activity of incoming and outgoing passengers and airport officials. The voices of announcers calling out flight numbers came over loudspeakers, the sharp clatter of heels across the vast floor; the subdued ringing of telephones, the muffled sound of the aircraft out there in the sunlight beyond the windows.

Edwin Gale poised alongside Dr. Morelle, one eye searching for the hire-car chauffeur who would be meeting him, while he kept his other eye on the tall, dark figure who had now moved slightly in front of him. Gale thought this was about the moment for him to say goodbye, and he gave a little cough and fixed a suitable smile on his face. His glance ranged over the spare angular frame in the beautifully-cut, dark blue pinstripe single-breasted suit, from the black, elegantly polished custom-built shoes to the inch of cream silk shirt cuffs and the negligently knotted bow tie of dark, polka-dotted silk beneath the firmly-chiselled chin. Gale eyed the gaunt features, whose greying temples were shadowed by the rakishly-slanting soft black hat.

But Dr. Morelle might not have noticed that the other was

still there; all his attention was concentrated on the scene before him; his gaze raked over the throng of people expectantly.

CHAPTER EIGHT

It was not the first time that Miss Frayle had been to London Airport, either to see people off or to meet them in. The last occasion, she had come to wave Dr. Morelle goodbye as he had disappeared along the gallery to the covered way and the waiting aircraft that would soon be bound for New York.

She had never been in an aircraft herself, with the exception of a flip in a little airplane one holiday at a seaside resort. Brief as the flight had been, she had been thankful when it was over and she found herself back on the ground again. The whole idea of flying made her nervous, and she never failed to envy and marvel at those who regarded flying to the other side of the world as no more remarkable than taking a taxi.

All the same, she was sure she would not have felt half so nervous if she were flying with Dr. Morelle. She wouldn't have minded going with him to New York, she'd told herself. She wouldn't mind flying to the moon with him. But there had been no necessity for her to go along with him on the trip, while there had been plenty of work she could catch up with here in London.

Now, as the uniformed driver swung the black Daimler past the airport entrance, and Miss Frayle took in with interest the great air terminal, where hundreds of aircraft with their crews and passengers of a dozen different nationalities landed and took off daily, spread its long, low symmetrical buildings beneath the morning sunshine.

It was exciting to welcome back Dr. Morelle a day earlier than she had expected, and already her heart was beating quickly and her mind began to feel dazzled at the sight of the airport. She hoped she would not be confused and go to the wrong place to meet him. She had already been a little put out by yesterday's cable, telling of his changed time of departure from New York. Dr. Morelle had not stated whether the time of arrival at London Airport was the same as it would have been originally. She had checked that it was, and she had ordered the car to call for her at Harley Street in good time, to ensure a generous margin on the right side.

But even now, early as she knew she was from the twentieth look at her wristwatch that morning, a sudden panic gripped her at the possibility that in some way she had bungled it and that Dr. Morelle had already arrived. A big limousine swept past her from the direction of the airport and involuntarily she threw it a look, as if expecting to see that sardonic face glaring at her from within. But it was only an elderly woman in the corner.

His plane couldn't have landed yet, she told herself. She had taken the precaution to call the airport before leaving to check that the flight was as scheduled. It was, she was reassured. It was due in on time. Even Dr. Morelle, Miss Frayle comforted herself, could not exert his influence, powerful and impelling as it was, to the extent of forcing the Stratocruiser to accelerate its speed so that it would come in well ahead of time, merely to spite her.

As her car proceeded at a low speed alongside the airfield, Miss Frayle idly followed the course of an airliner, as it took off and began to gain altitude. She watched it gleam in a wide sweep against the blue sky. She saw the entrance to the underground tunnel ahead which led under part of the concrete runways to the vast Terminal Area on the other side. They dipped down into the greyish, yellow floodlit, concrete cavity which seemed to Miss Frayle to run for an interminable length. Then the car was pointing upwards and they came out suddenly into the sparkling sunlight, into the heart of London Airport. One moment they had been underground in the eerie light, and now, with dramatic suddenness, a mass of steel, concrete, and glass rose up to greet the eye. Miss Frayle saw the lofty, glass-domed control tower dominating the scene, and then the car was purring along the wide, neat drive to the sprawling, many-windowed Passenger Reception Building.

'I'll park here,' the chauffeur said politely to Miss Frayle. A thought occurred to the man. 'But since you're in plenty of time, you may want to go to the Queen's Building? You can interest yourself there watching the planes going and coming.'

'All right,' Miss Frayle said, leaning forward to speak through the glass partition, which the chauffeur had drawn open. 'You'll wait?'

'That's right.' The other alighted smartly, opened the door, and Miss Frayle stood for a moment by the car, the throbbing sound of aircraft engines in her ears. With a smile at the chauffeur, she went through the doors of Passenger Reception. The low-ceiling, comparatively small entrance hall was quiet after the drumming of aircraft outside.

After a slight pause, Miss Frayle took the escalator to the first floor and the vast hall, which was the Main Concourse. She took in the lengths of counter, behind which were the various airline companies' personnel, bank offices, General Enquiries, against the background of the doors leading to the Customs beyond. In the spaces intending passengers sat, waiting in green leather armchairs, for the voice of the loudspeaker which would summon them to begin their journey.

Miss Frayle looked at her watch yet again, checked it with the clock by the great windows, found she really had half an hour in hand, glanced out of the windows, through which the sunlight streamed, and then she turned and went up the stairs to the next floor.

Here, a balcony lounge overlooked the busy scene below. Passengers who had arrived well in advance of their flight schedules sat chatting with friends. Miss Frayle passed the crescent of shops, her attention attracted casually by the variety of goods displayed. Pottery and toys, souvenirs and confectionery.

There was a bookstall and a hairdresser, telephone booths and a childrens' nursery.

Through the glass swing-doors at the end of the balcony, Miss Frayle went into the lounge bar and on to the passenger restaurant. Its tall windows looked over the great expanse of the airfield, and there was a wide terrace where people were watching the arrival and departure of the planes. She went out to see a large aircraft taxi in, glancing inevitably at her watch. No, this wasn't the one Dr. Morelle was on, still twenty-five minutes yet. Time enough to spend a little while in the Queen's Building.

She retraced her steps down to the Main Concourse and found the covered way to her objective. Now she had gained the spacious Exhibition Hall, and continued through it to the restaurant, where she was at once drawn to the windows overlooking the great expanse of runways and the ever-moving aircraft. The restaurant was fairly empty and Miss Frayle chose one of the window tables. She glanced round and saw a waiter approaching and sat down and ordered coffee. She relaxed and gazed through the huge window before her, which formed part of a long curve of more projecting, cantilevered windows ranging along all of one side of the restaurant.

Idly stirring her coffee, she watched a string of passengers below filing from the covered ramp out on to the apron, where a twin-engined airliner waited, its passenger door open. She wondered vaguely what its destination was. France, Switzerland, Scandinavia, or somewhere in the Mediterranean? It might be anywhere in the world, she supposed. She observed the plane again, with its one propeller either side of the fuselage indicating that is was powered by no more than two engines; and it occurred to her that it would not be engaged on the longer flights. She was reasoning that aircraft of the more powerful, four-engined type would be used to span global distances when a voice in her ear brought her up with a start.

'Why, hello, Miss Frayle?'

It was a shortish, middle-aged man wearing a black coat and

striped trousers, looking like a barrister's clerk, who stood there smiling at her warmly. She recognized him at once. He was, in fact, Jim Catchpole, chief crime reporter on the *Leader*. He was carrying the bowler hat and neatly-folded umbrella which had long made him a familiar figure in Fleet Street. Miss Frayle asked him to sit down, and he ordered a coffee. She refused his invitation to have some more herself.

'Don't tell me it's something sinister at London Airport which brings you here,' she said, with a little smile, watching him put lump after lump of sugar into his coffee.

'I was just about to ask you,' Jim Catchpole said, 'if there was something nasty in the woodshed. I mean, why else would you be here? I take it you're with Dr. Morelle?'

She explained that she was meeting Dr. Morelle off the plane from New York, while he nodded his head, recalling that he had done a piece in his paper at the time of Dr. Morelle's departure for the United States. He had previously spoken to him over the telephone to obtain the information about his lecture tour and the meetings he would be having with eminent American psychiatrists and criminologists. Then he was explaining to Miss Frayle the reason for his presence at the airport. It was a Sûreté detective he knew who'd made a quick trip to Scotland Yard and whom he'd just seen off back to Paris.

'I haven't met you,' he was saying, 'since that business at the drama school place last year. Though we've talked on the phone.' Miss Frayle nodded. 'It was just after that, wasn't it,' he said, 'when you went back to work for his nibs?'

Miss Frayle's mind was taken back to when she had been secretary to that tempestuous one-time stage star, Hugo Coltamn, at his dramatic school down in Surrey. Dr. Morelle's appearance on the scene in connection with a series of mysterious, dark events culminating in brutal murder had brought him into her orbit once more. Once more she had come under the old spell of his strange personality, and had gone back to work for him.

And, she admitted to herself, though she would never let Dr.

Morelle know it, she hadn't regretted her return to 221b Harley Street. True, he had soon exhibited that sardonic impatience plus signs of that somewhat twisted sense of humour from which she had suffered during the years she had first been in his employment. But, perhaps because she had grown more philosophic, or that his work was so tremendously absorbing, she had found him less of a rasping edge to her nerves.

'Still carrying a torch for him, eh, Miss Frayle?' Jim Catchpole's voice broke in upon her thoughts. She gazed at him with affected innocence over her horn-rimmed spectacles, but try as she might she failed to fight back the blush that swept over her face.

'I don't know what you mean,' she said, furious at herself for not being able to conceal an emotion which she tried so carefully to keep hidden away in the innermost recesses of her heart. The other had grinned at her mischievously, then turning away, with his hands clasped over the handle of his umbrella, he leaned forward to gaze down at the airfield. His pink brow was suddenly corrugated beneath his sandy, thinning hair, and he muttered half to himself:

'Something familiar about that chap, too.'

Miss Frayle, wondering vaguely what he was talking about, leaned forward to follow the direction of the other's gaze. 'Who?'

Jim Catchpole nodded to a straggle of passengers moving away from a large aircraft across the apron towards the passenger ramp. Miss Frayle had not noticed that the plane had been there before.

'See him?' the newspaperman said. 'Thickset chap walking just behind your boss. Now where have I seen him before—?'

But his conjectures were interrupted by a sharp yelp of dismay from Miss Frayle, who leapt to her feet so that the coffee cups rattled. For a moment she stood as if paralysed, transfixed by the sight of the great airliner, unmistakably four-engined, and the passengers from it, which included a tall, familiar figure. With a gabble of apologies she started for the door. Suddenly she remembered she hadn't paid the waiter and she stopped to fumble with her handbag. Jim Catchpole stopped her. 'Have it on me. You go and meet Dr. Morelle.'

Throwing him her grateful thanks, Miss Frayle bustled out of the restaurant and tore into the Exhibition Hall. She came up with a jerk, feverishly trying to recall the direction she should take. Her mind a confused whirl, she sped across to a wide staircase. Halfway down she hesitated again, then deciding this was the right way, hurried on.

Her heart pounding, she raced down the stairs. How could she have been so stupid? she kept asking herself. To have planned it all so carefully, so that she would arrive with plenty of time, then to let herself in for it like this. Of course it was Jim Catchpole's fault. If he hadn't come over and started talking to her, she would have kept her eyes on the time, and this panic would never have happened. Then ruefully she told herself she had no one but herself to blame. She ought to know how quickly time goes when the moments were unguarded.

Suddenly she saw a newsreel cinema in front of her, and with a gasp of horror realized she hadn't noticed it before. She was lost. She shouldn't have come down the stairs at all. Almost sobbing with vexation, she saw that the wide, unfamiliar glass doors which faced her obviously led outside. She turned back and shot upstairs to regain the Exhibition Hall. She dashed across it to the covered way, she was sure she recognized it as the way to the Main Concourse, which she had taken previously.

With a thankful gulp she found herself in the vast hall once more, a cool, crisp woman's voice announcing a flight number. This was the Main Concourse, where she was to meet Dr. Morelle.

Almost as she took in her bearings, the great expanse of windows, the lofty ceiling, she sighted him. At the other end of the hall. He had just emerged through the door from the Customs. As she sped towards him, miraculously avoiding a collision with a young couple turning away from one of the counters, she saw the man whom Jim Catchpole had pointed out to her in that brief instant before she had dashed away. He was just behind Dr. Morelle.

Dr. Morelle's gaze encountered her as she approached, remembering just in time, she hoped, to reduce her speed to walking pace. She did her best to appear casual, but her heart was pounding like a sledge hammer. The man behind said something to Dr. Morelle, so that he turned away from Miss Frayle for a moment. Then Dr. Morelle turned back to her, raising his black hat, and that faintly mocking smile twitched the corners of his mouth.

'For a moment,' he said, 'I thought I was going to be disappointed, that you wouldn't be here to meet me.'

'Why, Dr. Morelle,' she stammered breathlessly. 'As if I'd fail you. I've been waiting for you quite a little while.'

One dark eyebrow was raised quizzically at her. 'Really? By your state of near-physical collapse I imagined you must have only just got here in time. Perhaps your alarm clock let you down?'

As her eyes sparkled with mortification and she fought to control her breathlessness, he turned towards the man beside him, who was smiling at her gently. Miss Frayle took in his stocky figure, his fleshy, smooth features, the charming smile which became more brilliant so that it might have been switched on above the plump, somewhat weakish chin.

'Miss Frayle,' Dr. Morelle was saying, 'my invaluable secretary. This is Mr. Gale. We met on the plane.'

'Delighted to meet you,' Gale said.

Miss Frayle blinked, smiled back at him, and found she was breathing more steadily. 'How do you do,' she said.

CHAPTER NINE

Gale threw away his half-smoked cigarette as the hired limousine slid silently up beside him. The chauffeur quickly slipped out, took his bag, and opened the door. Gale sank back into the luxurious cushioning of the back seat. Absently he watched the chauffeur close the door, put his bag on the front seat, and slide behind the wheel. The car ghosted away from the terminal block and down into the tunnel, and a few seconds later was heading away from London Airport towards London on the A4.

Presently Gale lit another cigarette and relaxed. He could not help feeling in a self-congratulatory mood. He was recalling his goodbyes to Dr. Morelle and the young woman, Miss Frayle, and there was no doubt in his mind that he had made a favourable impression on her at any rate. Rather a sweet little thing, if a bit wide-eyed and fluttering. Not the sort of secretary he'd have expected Dr. Morelle to have. He would have imagined someone smarter, more efficient-looking. Still, she'd certainly taken him for the friendly, not unattractive man-of-the-world type.

Dr. Morelle, of course, was different. How he'd gone over with him, he wouldn't know. All the same, he felt confident he had made out all right with him. Gale's mind held some vague idea that his meeting with Dr. Morelle had provided him with an opening which he might put to good use at some later date. He wasn't at all sure how or when; it was just that he felt the future would provide him with an opportunity to benefit out of his encounter on the plane.

As they left the Great West Road and slowed into the traffic streams of Hammersmith, Gale let his mind range ahead with more immediate plans he envisaged. His first thought was a lazy half hour in his bath. Then an easy spell in his dressing gown with his feet up while he went through the mail that would have accumulated in his absence. His thoughts fastened upon business matters. He frowned to himself. He was wondering about the individual who was to be the object of his first call, as soon as he'd rested up for an hour or two at the flat. He'd make it after lunch, he thought.

After some traffic hold-ups in Kensington, the car turned off into the Park where, although the pace was leisurely, it was continuous. Gale lounged back enjoying the sunshine and the bright green leafiness flanking the carriageway, and now his ruminations revolved about the woman J.K. had called Dolores. His hand wandered to his notecase and he took out the piece of paper on which J.K. had scribbled her address and telephone number. Dolores del Robia. Spanish, probably. If that was her real name. It conjured up for him a swaying, voluptuous figure with a warm, ripe mouth and dark inviting eyes. He found himself tingling with pleasurable anticipation at the meeting, there might be a little fun to be had out of it, as well as business.

He looked up as the car stopped at the gates leading into Park Lane. Two or three minutes and he would be in his flat. The traffic cop waved them on and they turned left, then right into a side street, to slow to a stop outside the unobtrusive entrance of Parkside House.

As Gale went into the cool, discreetly-lit entrance hall, the uniformed porter hurried to take his luggage, and opened the lift doors for him. The lift zoomed noiselessly up to the third floor, and Gale got out and went along a carpeted corridor. He opened the flat door. The porter took the luggage in. Gale entered the familiar entrance lobby. The double glass doors opening into the lounge bathed the lobby in sunlight. He stepped into the large, long windowed room.

He looked around with a sigh of contentment, as the porter

went out. It was good to be home. The familiar luxury of the place flowed over him. The apple-green shade of carpet and upholstery harmonized with the gilt chairs and settee, and the sun-bronzed curtains at the wide windows. The small, expensive chandelier hanging from the plaster-carved ceiling, the polished Sheraton table. The gleaming candelabra, the cut-glass decanters on their silver tray on the long, low table beneath the round carved mirror.

Gale crossed to the windows. He opened them so that the murmur of traffic down there in Park Lane seeped into the room. But the sound was not obtrusive and the air wafting in across Hyde Park was fresh. He moved back to the double glass doors and almost unconsciously his hand wandered down to the ivory-coloured telephone on the small table. He dialled and waited expectantly. The burr-burr in his ear stopped.

'Hello?'

The soft husky voice was lazily seductive. It was her, all right. He was sure of that. But on a sudden impulse, he couldn't explain why, he didn't answer. The voice came again. Still lazy and insinuating, so that his heartbeat quickened. He still didn't answer, instead he slowly returned the telephone to its cradle. For some moments he stood there staring at the telephone, a little smile on his face. Her voice confirmed the picture he had conjured up in the car. Puzzling a little over the sudden quirk which had inexplicably caused him to hang up on her, he went over to the sideboard and poured himself a drink.

Edwin Gale lunched leisurely at the Ritz, taking his time, enjoying the coolness of the restaurant, the greenness of the trees outside the windows, savouring the pleasure of being back in London, after the heat and bustle of New York. He took his time over coffee and then went out into Piccadilly, walked a little way in the direction of Hyde Park before taking a taxi to Chelsea.

The taxi drew up a short distance from where the Bookworm sign stuck out over the pavement at the World's End part of the King's Road, Chelsea. The shop beneath the sign comprised a basement full of books, a ground floor full of books and the two upper stories full of books. Everywhere the visitor turned were mountains of books; topsy-turvy leaning towers spilled on to rickety tables and were spread on the floor under the tables; books sprawled on odd pieces of furniture. A sagging sofa, kitchen chairs, bedroom chairs, armchairs, while round the rough unpainted walls shelves groaned beneath the weight of books.

Outside the shop crammed trays and boxes were labelled with bargains from a penny to a shilling a volume, and books were stacked haphazardly on the pavement. Inside the shop attempts were made to inform prospective customers of the sections where they might be expected to find the title they were in search of. But these directions, scrawled on the backs of envelopes or bits of cardboard pinned to the shelves, were inclined to be misleading. The never-ending stream of book-lovers, browsing readers and would-be purchasers circulating round the shop at all hours, were mostly forgetful when it came to returning to its proper section the book they had picked up to sample.

Gale paused outside the shop for a moment to survey the not unfamiliar confusion with an expression of slight distaste. The sight of a knot of scruffy characters picking over the tattered volumes didn't appeal to him overmuch. He preferred people and things to be clean and neat and orderly. He came in from the bright sunshine and clamour of the buses and traffic of the King's Road into the musty, dusty, comparative silence of this world of books, whose pungent smell smarted in his nostrils. He noted a bespectacled, unwashed-looking young man and an untidy, middle-aged, grey-faced woman, who were assistants, and he asked the woman if Mr. Outram was about. The woman nodded towards the darkness at the back of the shop, and Gale picked his way round the customers and over the stacks of books until he came to a short dark passage. It led past a shelf on which reposed a dirty washbasin and gas ring, to a door which was ajar.

He pushed the door open, and a thin-faced man with wispy hair above a bulbous forehead looked up at him over steel-rimmed spectacles. His eyes, which were faded, pale, and held an expression of perpetual disillusionment, widened a little.

'Good afternoon,' he said, 'this is an unexpected pleasure. I thought you were still in the land of liberty and the free, on the other side of the heaving main.'

Gale had deliberately not telephoned Outram that he intended to look in on him. His purpose was to convey to the other that his call was nothing more than a passing visit, and that business had little part in it. There was not much those pale eyes behind the steel spectacles didn't pick up, but at least Gale didn't intend to make it easy for him.

'Got back this morning,' Edwin Gale said casually, placing his Malacca cane on the small, untidy desk behind which Outram had risen at his entrance. 'I happened to be this way, and thought I'd drop in on you.' He peeled off his chamois gloves as the other without saying anything, pushed a packet of cigarettes across to him. He took a cigarette and lit it himself. Outram didn't smoke. He kept them only for his friends and customers, he said.

'I hope you had a pleasant trip,' Outram said, after Gale had sat carefully in a wobbly, cane-backed chair. 'Not to say a profitable one.'

'I did all right. It was nice to get away for a break.'

'I'd like to go to the U.S. myself, don't suppose I will though.'

Gale gazed through a cloud of cigarette smoke at the dilapidated office. Here again stacks of books of all kinds climbed precariously against the walls from floor to ceiling. Only the space which was occupied by a dirty unwashed window, overlooking a small back yard, was not obscured by volumes.

Outram had sat down again in his squeaking, swivel chair, while Gale, deciding after all not to trust the chair he had taken, pushed aside a clutter of books on the corner of the desk and leaned against it.

'I think you'd like it,' he said in answer to the other's observation.

'You flew, I suppose?' Gale nodded. 'That I'd never do, a nice big boat for me.'

'Flying's all right,' Gale said. 'Saves a hell of a lot of time.' Then he drew his brows together in a little frown as if he had suddenly been reminded of something. 'Talking of America,' he said slowly, 'reminds me. You remember that little job you showed me just before I went?'

Outram's pale, bulging forehead wrinkled in furrows of cogitation for a few moments before he answered. 'The Columbus job?'

This was the moment. Gale took a deep drag at his cigarette and expelled a spiral of smoke abstractedly. For a few seconds it seemed as if he was not going to pursue the subject, he might have forgotten even having mentioned it. Then: 'What were you asking for it,' Gale said.

'The price hasn't gone up,' the other said, 'or down.'

Gale looked as disinterested as he could. 'It doesn't matter,' he said. 'I just don't recall what you were asking for it.'

'Two-fifty quid,' said Outram with a smile as if this was a transparent lie. 'In case you were thinking in dollars.'

'Isn't that a bit pricey?' Gale said, tapping the ash off his cigarette.

'It's worth four times as much. To the right buyer.'

It was, too, as Gale knew well enough. When Outram had first shown it to him, he had at once realized that it was a beautifully done job. The work of a craftsman, painstakingly and lovingly carried out. The chap must have been a bit of a genius in his way.

Gale was recalling that at the time, although he hadn't got enough proof, that the gifted character responsible for this exquisite work of art had about a year before been removed from the scene of his activities. It was only a vague whisper which had reached him over the underworld grapevine. But apparently he was doing a stretch. The result of another example of his handiwork being brought to light and subjected to the pitiless scrutiny associated with police investigation. Which scrutiny had revealed that the item in question was a fake. A clever fake, undoubtedly, but a fake.

What this meant was that the major portion of the £250 which Outram was asking for this present job would go into his own pocket. The artist languishing in clink might have the satisfaction of learning that his wife, or the woman who went under that description, would collect £20 or £30, no more, to ease her lot while the breadwinner was absent.

Every fibre of Gale's being recoiled from the thought of putting £200 into the pocket of the bespectacled little man who sat there regarding him with a look of benign mildness, simply for having performed the relatively simple task of acting as go-between for the craftsman who'd done all the work and brought his consummate skill and expert knowledge into play with such alluringly impressive results. Gale had hoped that since he refused to pay the price when the item had first been offered to him prior to his departure for America, the figure asked would have slumped a trifle now. After all, there wasn't all that number of operators engaged in the same line of business as he was himself, who would be interested in such a specialized piece of fakery.

In fact, at the time he had been quite frank when he had argued with Outram that it wasn't worth the money, because he hadn't a market in mind for it. And the other had answered not to worry, and that he would put it by against the chance that Gale would find a potential client for this line of goods. Gale had thought then that Outram would have it on his hands for a long time, until he would ultimately job it off with a lot of other junk, or something.

But his meeting with J.K. had altered all that; now it appeared that Outram had been possessed of not a little prescience, or at any rate, shrewdness, banking on his knowledge that, although the market for it was admittedly small, the item was of such brilliant workmanship that it must inevitably find a purchaser who would find a way to make a very good use of it.

Gale gave a little sigh. This was how it had worked out anyway. J.K. had given him a signal light, whose beam had aimed itself straight at Outram's musty, ramshackle bookshop in the King's Road. He eyed the other with a certain amount of distaste. 'Can I see it again?'

Outram gave him a little smile, stood up unhurriedly from the desk and crossed to the door, his feet shuffling in the carpet slippers that he wore. 'You haven't been able to find another customer for it?' Gale said meaningly.

The pale eyes regarded him over the spectacles from the door.

'Funny thing,' Outram said, 'but I knew you'd be back for it. So I kept it for you.'

'Very kind of you, I'm sure,' Gale said, and didn't go easy with the sarcasm.

The other smiled at him blandly, and Gale heard his shuffling footsteps ascending the dark creaking stairs to the floor above. There behind locked doors would be the hiding place wherein the main source of the bookseller's livelihood was secreted. Erotic literature by old and modern authors; richly illustrated volumes on the same theme; sumptuously bound, or dog-eared and cheaply produced. And those samples of the book-faker's, such as the one in which Gale was interested.

Edwin Gale waited glancing idly round at the mass of books surrounding him, which provided the owner of the Bookworm with a meagre livelihood on the one hand, and on the other a cover for his less respectable and more lucrative activities. He wondered idly if the little bookseller, with his eccentric front which he so studiously cultivated, had ever been rumbled by the police. He had never heard of him ever having been pinched, but then he knew very little about him. Except that he kept his trap shut.

His ruminations were interrupted by Outram's scuffling return, with a small, dirty, brown-paper parcel. He blew a film of dust off it which caused Gale to wonder if it had been kept on some shelf with a batch of other volumes, so that he could not help speculating further upon the possibility of other similar treasures which the dusty rooms upstairs might hold.

His attention fixed itself on the parcel which Outram was now slowly untying with fumbling, dirty fingers. After a few moments he unwrapped it. Gale picked up the volume that lay revealed, handling it carefully, his eyes gleaming with a kind of awesome appreciation. As before he found it difficult to believe that it was not in fact the genuine article. Gently, he turned the yellowed, spotted pages, worn and tattered at the edges, for all the world as if by the passage of years, and the vicissitudes of travel which the thing was supposed to have suffered since it had left the hands of its original owner. Every detail seemed to have been attended to, not a flaw was apparent to him.

He felt himself transported back to the big, airless, sun-filled room of the house at Falmouth, with J.K. and his white teeth and his multi-coloured shirt and bronzed, hairy chest. J.K., who had slapped the old whaling logbook onto the wide, shiny desk. Who had kicked this whole business off, and who this time wasn't even going to collect his ten percent on the deal.

Presently Gale looked up to glance at Outram, who seemed to be engrossed with business correspondence at the littered desk. He did not raise his eyes until Gale closed the volume with a faint snap. He looked up, his pale gaze only vaguely questioning over his steel-rimmed spectacles

'All right,' Gale said, 'I'll take it.'

CHAPTER TEN

The sound of the telephone shrilled into the smallish, luxurious bedroom, and with a shrug of annoyance Dolores del Robia halted the application of the mascara brush to her long, thick eyelashes. For an exasperated moment she stared at herself in the ornate dressing table mirror.

What she saw there filled her with a certain amount of satisfaction. Although she was only halfway through putting on her makeup, she calculated her age would have been difficult to assess. Twenty-seven or thirty? No more, she assured herself. The high cheek bones and the creamed skin gave her a slightly harsh appearance, but she would smooth that away with cunningly applied tint and shading. Her eyes were round and dark, and gave a curious impression that shadows lay in the depths of the pupils. She touched the few, fine lines beneath the eyes, and smiled a little ruefully at her reflection. Her mouth was full, but there was a weakness about her lower lip.

The insistent burr-burr made her reach for a wrap behind her on the bed, and as she pulled it round her, the mirror caught the lines of flesh that were beginning to thicken her magnificent figure. Beneath her black lace panties and brassiere the muscles of calf and thigh, back and shoulders, rippled her bronzed skin. But now she was turned away from the dressing table. Her thoughts were held by the jangling telephone. Her smooth brow creased as she wondered who it was ringing her.

Shaking out the rich waves of her black hai,r she went out of the bedroom's dark-gold décor, into the sitting room and picked up the telephone.

Her voice had the same husky tone that the man at the other end had heard earlier, though this time it contained an edge of impatience, instead of almost languorous indifference.

'My name is Gale,' she heard him say. 'Edwin Gale. You won't know me, but a mutual friend and—ah—business associate suggested I contact you.'

A pencilled eyebrow raised slightly, a gleam of curiosity appeared in her eyes. 'You intrigue me, Mr. Gale, just a little. Who's this mutual pal you mention?'

'J.K.'

She gave a sudden intake of breath. There was a little pause. 'Is he in London?'

'No. I tied up a deal with him before I took off from New York. I just got in this morning. He suggested we should get to know each other.'

She was about to say something, and then she decided against it. Her dark eyes became thoughtful, the lines of her face were suddenly harshened, as if her thoughts were not altogether filled with the milk of human kindness. 'When am I to have the pleasure?' was all she said. The edge in her voice was replaced by a practised tantalizing note.

'He said for me to make it the sooner, the better.' Gale paused. She made no reply. She was waiting for him to take it a step further. 'He seemed to think we should find quite a thing or two in common,' he said.

'What kind of proposition have you got in mind, Mr. Gale?'

'I think you'll agree it's one you'll be interested in.'

She let a husky chuckle ripple along the line to his ear. 'What's my cut to be?'

He gave a little laugh. 'It's nice to meet someone so business-like. Especially someone who, as I've been given to understand, is so attractive as you are.'

'I believe in starting off as I mean to go along,' she said. 'That's if I decide to go along.'

He made his voice sound brisk. 'When could we talk it over?

This evening, for example? I'd be pleased to see you any time at all. Anywhere you say.'

She glanced at the expensive-looking travelling clock that stood beside the telephone. 'I have to go out to dinner. But if you'd like to drop along for a drink around six-thirty, I'll be around. We could chin things over for a cosy half hour.'

'I'd like that,' he said.

'You may,' she said. 'Depends on what you've got on your mind whether I will.'

She told him how to get to her, then she let the receiver drop slowly on to its cradle and she leaned back, against the doorway to the bedroom. Her eyes were half-closed; she was musing over the confident, worldly voice over the wire which had suddenly jerked back into her memory the image of J.K. She was smiling faintly, bitterly. J.K's dolls never lasted long. But they took on the game with their peepers wide open. You had to give him that. He'd made it clear about that. They had their little day and went. No regrets. No strings. It was fun while it was fun, and J.K. and his dolls always said *adieu* still pals.

She pulled her wrap round her bronzed firm shoulders, and sauntered slowly on her spike heels over to the array of bottles and cut-glass decanters stacked on the low chest back of the corduroy-covered, button-backed settee. She poured herself a large gin and French. She sipped it first, rolling the spirit round her tongue as if tasting the bouquet of an expensive wine. Then she tipped the glass and tossed the remainder down her throat. She went into the bedroom and sat down at the dressing table and picked up the mascara brush again.

She did a good job on her face, and when she was through she really took a good view of what she saw in the mirror. She put on a deep rose, three-quarter-length dinner dress. It was a beautifully-cut dramatic number, with a wide, heart-shaped neckline, low. She surveyed her reflection in the long, gilt wall mirror, twisting around critically. Smiling, she returned to the dressing table for her perfume.

She went into the sitting room, took a cigarette from a heavy silver cigarette box and lit it. She poured herself another drink, and stood by the window staring out at the mews, which was beginning to fill with the shadows of approaching dusk. It was quiet, that was the thing she liked about the place, it was quiet. It was shabby and dilapidated-looking, not like some of the mews in the vicinity, which were fashionably dolled up, the flats picked out in pinks or blues, with lanterns and wrought-iron gates, and the rest. The stairs leading to her front door could do with a coat of paint, the front door itself could use some paint also, but where she was it was the only flat. She liked it that way.

She stared over her glass at a cat that made its leisurely way across the untidy space below, while she wondered what sort of man was this Edwin Gale. He sounded middle-aged and sure of himself. But then, most of the middle-aged men she knew sounded sure of themselves. They all wanted the same thing, so that simplified their angle of approach to some extent, that gave their one-track minds a steady, plodding course to follow. They were sure enough, all right.

A faint smile touched her mouth. But this Edwin Gale sounded as if he was going to be different. He had a proposition of a different kind that was bothering him. Where did J.K. come into the picture? She would be somewhat intrigued to learn about that. Not that it mattered. She couldn't care less about J.K. or any other man, come to think of it. It was money that mattered. It was money she had to make stick to her fingers while she could. While her face and figure still had what it takes.

She wondered idly if, perhaps, this was something a bit different that was on the cards. Different from what she'd been working the past few years. She blew a cloud of cigarette smoke that spiralled up from a protruding lower lip.

She had kicked off when she was only fifteen. There had been the scandal at the expensive school she'd been sent to, which had resulted in her having to leave. Her mother, who was divorced, and had to have the sun and fun of Cannes to make life bearable, had packed her off to live with an aunt in Sussex. Then there'd been funny business with the aunt's middle-aged cousin, an army type, and she'd come to London on her own, but with £500, which the cousin had paid to her to keep her pretty mouth shut. She'd learned fast how easy it was to wheedle money out of men, especially middle-aged and old men. Preferably old men: she made them feel young again.

She had looked much older than her years, and took advantage of this at the appropriate moment. She had taken the trouble to acquaint herself with the Criminal Law Amendment Act, 1885, and the Children and Young Persons Act, 1933. Which knowledge she was not unwilling to display whenever necessary to enforce her demands.

Her thirst for knowledge, which would be useful to her in squeezing money out of men, led her to become a student of the financial columns of the newspapers. That way she picked up news about who was in the money; or she would seek her prospective victim from the pages of *Kelly's Street Directory* or the *Directory of Directors*, *Who's Who*, or *Debrett*. Occasionally her ambitions soared higher and the *Almanach de Gotha* became a source of information.

That way she had got herself a fabulous six weeks at Monte Carlo, and as a result of that there had been Rome last summer and Venice in the autumn. But mostly she played it in London. She felt safer amongst local big business city tycoons; or, for a change of pace, the aristocratic old sports up from their estates and crumbling mansions to forget taxation and death duties for fun and games in Mayfair and Soho. She had been lucky. There'd been several narrow squeaks when a victim had threatened to squawk instead of paying up that last rich bite. Yes, there'd been some rough moments, but she'd got away with it. She'd found that it was being ruthless always paid off. Never weaken, that was the gag. No matter how they sobbed or grovelled at her feet, never be kidded into going soft-hearted. J.K. had admired her for that. He was as tough as they came, and it was a quality he'd liked in her. If only she'd been able to hang on to the loot, that was the one flaw in her makeup. She couldn't save money. She admitted it, and she still couldn't do anything about it. That old rainy day stuff had never meant anything to her. As it came in, so it went out. Fast.

She was ruminating over her current meal ticket, a big business type in detergents, with an avaricious glint that narrowed her round, dark eyes, when the doorbell buzzed.

She glanced at the exquisite diamond wristwatch on her smooth wrist. Was it forty-five minutes since he'd telephoned? She'd been a long way in that time, a long journey down memory lane. A round trip sparked by his recalling J.K. to her mind. She lit another cigarette and knocked back the drink with a grimace. This egg who called himself Edwin Gale was ringing her doorbell—she latched her thoughts onto the here and now. What was the proposition he had, and where did J.K. fit? He didn't go in for giving prizes away, even for old time's sake. Why should he put anything in her way?

Yet she'd like a deal that was safe and easy with a fat killing at the payoff. Could it be that the stranger at her door who sought her cooperation really had something to offer? She stubbed the lipsticked butt of her cigarette into an ashtray, and smiled. It wasn't a particularly pleasant smile.

The buzz-buzz at the door again. She took her time smoothing her dress and giving her hair the once-over in the Murano mirror. Then she moved languorously to the door.

CHAPTER ELEVEN

Edwin Gale was deciding that whatever picture of her he had conjured up in his mind, Dolores del Robia in the flesh had certainly not let him down. Whichever way you looked at her, and he hadn't missed a curve of her, she was a strikingly attractive woman. And there was about her dark lustrous beauty that feminine mystery which he liked to associate with the warm-hearted, hot-blooded women of the alluring South.

Her husky-voiced invitation had confirmed the smile of welcome on her red mouth, and he had followed her into the sitting room. He had taken it all in; like the occupant, he thought, it was warm and cosy. It was tastefully, if a little exotically, furnished. As mews flats went he thought it was quite sumptuous. He liked the gay, gold-tinted pattern of the wallpaper; the low, well-cushioned settee beneath the pink-shaded, richly carved, gilt-and-cream lamp was inviting. The bottles, decanters, and glasses arranged on the low Spanish chest made a comforting sight, too.

He noted the two doors opening off the sitting room, and he supposed they led to the bedroom and the kitchen and bathroom. But his eyes only flickered round; they were watching greedily the seductive lines of figure as she stood by the drinks chest.

'What will you drink, Mr. Gale?'

'What do you suggest might be good for me? But I go for whisky this time of the evening.' He smiled, and added lightly: 'My name's Edwin.'

She lowered her eyelashes and began to juggle with a decanter and a glass.

'I should have remembered,' she said. 'Say when?'

He nodded and she squirted the siphon into a generous whisky.

'That'll do,' he said. 'Fine.'

She passed him the glass and poured herself a gin and French. He opened his gold cigarette case and offered her a cigarette. She took one, and he flicked his lighter into flame.

'Here's to us and mutual profit,' she said over the rim of her glass.

He raised his glass and they drank.

She lay back on the settee, crossing her long legs so that they showed to advantage. She patted the cushions beside her and her dark eyes sparkled.

'Make yourself cosy, Edwin,' she said. 'You've got a lot to unload off your big, manly chest.'

As he lowered himself down beside her, he let his eyes linger over the generous display of sun-bronzed flesh that curved its way under the low neckline of her dress. When he looked up into her face, her eyes were staring frankly into his, and there was a faint curl to her lips. He felt a little foolish, and he looked away and tried to appear absorbed with his drink.

She said: 'This proposition you were giving me over the phone. What's in it for me? And just to be nosey, how does my old dear pal J.K. come into it?'

Gale took a long drag at his cigarette and puffed a cloud of smoke up into the lampshade. 'A couple of days ago I paid him a call down in Cape Cod,' he said. 'We were winding up a little business. Then he mentioned someone named Lang. He said he thought I was right up his alley. He said you knew him.'

The large dark eyes were narrowed.

'What's your racket?'

He grinned at her and flicked the ash, a little over-casually into the ashtray at his elbow. 'I'm a dealer in books mostly. Old Books. Rare books. First editions. Expensive books.'

She nodded. 'I catch on,' she said. 'He really goes like crazy for what you could have to offer. The way he looked to me, anything on yellowed, musty paper with foreign writing or too illegible to read was all you needed to shove under his nose and he couldn't wait to get his money out. Only, I imagine he can't be that easy to take. He must know when to come out of the rain sometimes.' She paused, eyeing him intently. 'Why, you got something lined up?'

'That's what I'm here about,' he said.

'It could be he's ripe,' she said. 'Though I don't know for sure just what size of a mug the chump is. I've got to warn you about that.'

'Thanks for the tip,' he said. 'But the way it is, I think I've got something that would fool an expert. The only thing is, provided he doesn't get too much time to sort the goods over.'

'Which is where I come in,' she said, 'to take his mind off his work?'

'I agree it would be difficult for any man to concentrate on anything with you around,' he said. 'Except you.'

She didn't say anything. A wisp of cigarette smoke curled from her lips and spiralled upwards. 'I could take care of that department. But you haven't told me about J.K. Where he fits in. I've had no tip-off from him about you. We haven't been in touch for quite a while. I don't lie under his sunshade anymore.'

Gale suddenly thought of J.K's ten percent cut. Of how he'd said he'd get in touch with Dolores, of his confidence that she would collect for him. Gale supposed J.K. hadn't calculated he would contact Dolores so fast on his return to London, before she'd heard from him. That she'd be hearing from him any day was definite. Gale wondered if he could take advantage of J.K's delay in communicating with Dolores. If she'd been as shabbily treated by J.K. as he had, he thought, maybe she'd think again before following his instructions. Gale said: 'He'd improved on the sunshade last time I saw him. Got a canopied hammock. He was making good use of it.'

She took a gulp at her glass and grimaced as if there was a

bitter taste in the drink, and for a moment her eyes held a glint in their depths. 'What's his cut?'

'Ten percent. For putting me onto you. You'll collect for him,' he said. Gale paused and leaned slightly towards her. 'But maybe you don't feel so generous to J.K.?' Her eyes were wide now, looking into his and he saw the curious depth of the irises. 'Maybe,' he went on tentatively, 'you and I could come to some little arrangement between ourselves about that ten percent?'

She was staring into her glass, as if it held the secret of a seer's crystal. 'Maybe we could,' she said slowly, still contemplating the drink. 'Depends.'

Gale paused with his own glass halfway to his lips, and glanced at her sharply. Had he misjudged it? Had he taken it too fast? He ought to have waited, weighed her up more and how she felt about J.K. Then he told himself there was no point in saving it for another time. He had no intention of kicking in any cut to J.K. This time he was going to score off J.K.

'Depends,' he said. 'On what?'

She put a hand on his arm.

'My cut, Edwin, of course,' she said. 'In this wicked world a girl's got to think of what's in it for herself.'

Gale laughed and finished his drink. 'You're the star attraction,' he said easily. 'You can fix me good with Lang. I'll be frank with you,' he said. 'Without you, where would I be? You're the key to the set-up. No you, no Lang. No Lang, no loot. You'll have earned your percentage, and it won't be ten percent I'm thinking of for you.'

'What would you be thinking of for me?'

His expression was smooth, his slow smile was meant to be disarming. 'What would I be thinking of for you?'

'Your hearing's good.'

'I was going to cut you in a quarter of the take.' He paused. 'Twenty-five percent.'

'I don't need any hearing aid either.'

His smile was a little stiff. 'Or thirty-five percent if we lose J.K.'

She didn't answer. She held up her empty glass. 'Edwin,' she said. 'It needs a refill. And give one to yourself.'

He stubbed out his cigarette and he went over to the drinks, filled both glasses, and returned to the settee. He lit her fresh cigarette for her and his own, and picked up his drink.

'Here's to successful teamwork,' he said, and moved a little closer. He was experiencing a little difficulty reminding himself that he was there on a strictly business basis. He was feeling relaxed, now that she had agreed to his terms with, it seemed, complete satisfaction. The doubts that had hovered at the back of his mind before their meeting, that she might have played it tough and grasping had evaporated. The languorous appeal in her eyes suggested to him that she was not only happy about their business partnership, but that she might even be interested in operating on a more intimate level.

It was all very flattering; then he told himself he must not let it go to his head. Maybe she was irresistible, but business must come first. He took a long time over his drink, and then started in asking her questions about Lang. How had she met him? What was he like? When he would be in London? Where he would be staying?

From her replies, cautious as they were, he figured she had kept tabs on Lang's movements pretty thoroughly. She had first met him in Rome in the summer. Gale wondered what she'd been doing in Rome, but she didn't volunteer any explanation. Lang, she said, was pushing fifty. He was quiet, looked and acted a bit like some absent-minded professor. He didn't look particularly loaded. It just seemed to Dolores that anything he wanted he had, and he was crazy about rare books. The prospect, she was convinced, of possessing the relic so closely associated with the discoverer of America would have him ready and willing to dish out the cash, and no mistake. 'Just as a matter of being nosey,' she said, 'how much is the thing worth?'

'The genuine article? Priceless. But I thought I wouldn't be too greedy. My price is twenty thousand quid.'

'How reasonable can you get?' she said.

But she was nodding her dark head slowly, her eyes were glowing at the thought of it. He thought he could hear her brain working out thirty percent.

'If he likes the job,' she said, 'it'll be cash on the line. The money will be there.'

Gale's mouth went dry. This looked like being the easiest pickings of his career. He took another drink and a warning note sounded somewhere at the back of his mind. He would have to look out for snags. When anything looked so smooth and easy as this looked, he told himself, you had to watch out.

Dolores had stood up and he watched her with undisguised admiration as she went over and opened a drawer and took out a diary. She leafed through a few pages and paused. 'He is due in London the day after tomorrow,' she said, through a cloud of cigarette smoke. 'He'll be staying at Curzon's Hotel. He always stays there. Quiet place in Half Moon Street.' He nodded. He knew Curzon's. 'How long he'll hang around,' she said, 'I wouldn't know for certain. But it'll only be a few days, then takes off for home, sweet home.' She came back and sat down beside him again. He eyed the seductive curve of her legs. Then he turned to her over the rim of his glass.

'So?' he said, 'what's the first approach?'

'I'll take care of it,' she said confidently. 'What I suggest is that you throw a little party at your place. Just a few handpicked pals who'll impress him. I'll bring the chump along, with maybe one or two others. I'll put him wise who you are, and plant that you've got something to show him that he might care to give the once-over. It's all yours from then on.'

Gale's smooth face creased in a grin.

'I'll leave it to you to fix the date.'

'Give him a couple of days with his feet on the ground,' she said. 'I'll keep in touch and we'll set the trap when he's ripe.'

They finished their drinks and suddenly Gale felt it was time to go. He was reluctant to move. She was staring at him, and he thought he could see an amused glint in her dark eyes. As if she was waiting for him to make the first move. She uncrossed her legs, and one brushed against his own legs. Impulsively he leaned over and kissed her on the mouth. There was a momentary response and then she pushed him gently away. Her smile was friendly, teasing.

'Work and fun don't go together, Edwin,' she said softly. 'We want to keep our heads clear. So let's wait until the caper's through.'

CHAPTER TWELVE

As soon as he had gone Dolores curled up on the settee with another drink. She smoked a cigarette, her mind coldly turning over her visitor's remarkable proposition.

The man himself had little to attract her. Typically middle-aged, conceited, and no less amorously inclined than all the others, a factor she had always put to good advantage. Probably been quite handsome once, but now he was fighting a losing battle; he couldn't conceal the toll age and dissipation were wreaking.

His clothes were well-tailored, and he carried himself in a manner that almost succeeded in disguising the fact that he had a paunch. And he was doing all right. He'd just flown back from America. He had a flat in Park Lane. She didn't dislike him. She couldn't afford to—for a time. She must accept his little advances, encourage them—up to a point. If she played her cards well, he was going to be a money spinner.

She was certain Lang would bite. She was equally certain she could lead him to the bait. Although he seemed more interested in his stuffy collection than in the opposite sex, she flattered herself he hadn't been altogether blind to her feminine attractions. In a mild way. She'd kept tabs on him ever since, because big fish didn't swim into her net so often; but she thought the opportunity might come to hook him good and proper. It had. This was it.

Although they had not been in touch with each other for some time, she didn't doubt he'd be pleased to see her when he arrived in London. He'd told her so just before she'd left Rome.

Her part in the act was quite simple; but it was important. Her train of thought jerked to a stop as if her sudden frown was a danger signal.

She sipped her drink slowly.

If it was so important, maybe her cut should have been bigger. Gale had the goods and he was going to put over the deal; but he wouldn't get that far without her cooperation. Lang was staying only a few days. Without her initiative Gale would never have time to introduce himself to the American or get to work on him. Gale didn't know the man from Adam and could spend a lot of valuable time trying to find him. She was going to hand him over on a plate. She'd suggested the routine on the spot: the party: Yet she'd calmly accepted a less than a third cut.

She banged her glass down on the table and jerked to her feet. Peevishly she lit a fresh cigarette. She began pacing up and down.

Dolores del Robia, she told herself, you're slipping.

What was she going to do about it? She paused suddenly, her fingers nervously drumming the back of a chair. She hadn't protested maybe because at the back of her mind she had other ideas. She had led Gale to believe that his terms were okay; that she was willing to string along on the percentage basis. It wouldn't do to alert him if she had other ideas. Ideas like scooping the pool, for instance.

A sardonic smile twisted her full, curved mouth. Her eyes were dark malevolent crevices above the high cheekbones. She took a long drag at her cigarette and watched the expelled cloud of smoke curl into a huge question mark beneath the ceiling. Why not? Why not scoop the pool? Gale was a crook. He meant nothing to her.

It wasn't a question of what was so wrong in double-crossing him. How? That was the question. How to get her hands on the major share of the cash without arousing his suspicions? Time was short. She wasn't likely to have a chance of getting hold of this relic, this old fake book thing he'd yattered about, on her own. And once she'd got Lang to the party it would be too late.

She could visualize it. Gale would draw the wealthy bird away from the other guests. Take him to a quiet room, show him the fake, and spout a lot of nonsense. Presumably the deal would be clinched then and there. Later would come her reward. He'd dole out her thirty percent.

Another thought hit her. Would he? Was there any guarantee she'd get as much as that, or anything at all? She didn't know him. How far could she trust him? The only recommendation she had was J.K. had sent him. What was that worth? It certainly wasn't worth the ten percent J.K. was demanding, and she'd see he didn't get it.

She began pacing the floor again, her mind a cauldron. If she didn't get in first, Gale would, and she'd find he'd beat it with the kitty. She had no conscience about it now. The doubt she had suddenly created of Gale's true intentions continued to flash, like a neon sign, in her mind. She was convinced he'd double-cross her; equally convinced that she wasn't going to let him get away with it. But how to forestall him?

There appeared to be no time and no room for any tricky manœuvre. She had no legitimate reason to visit Gale's flat before the party. Would there be an opportunity to strike then? If so, in what way? The only way she could see was to grab the fake herself, before Lang got it.

But she couldn't do it herself. That wasn't her line.

She crushed the butt of her cigarette into the ashtray as a ray of hope dawned in her mind. Of course, she had told Gale she would bring Lang and probably a friend or two along. He would accept any friend of hers without comment. He'd have no time to entertain a suspicion of doubt, anyway. He would be concentrating exclusively on Lang. She would have the advantage, and so would whoever she took with her for the purpose. As this occurred to her so did the man for the job.

Vere Spencer.

Young and good-looking with the gloss to give him the air of the rich, gay man-about-town, he was crazy about her. He was basically a worthless character, except for such a break as this. Always hard-up, ready to consider any proposition that offered little risk and some reward. He scraped along on his wits, and in view of his pecuniary position, she had to admit that to herself, she couldn't regard them very highly. But they could work out a line of action together.

Her glance came to rest on the telephone as these thoughts chased through her mind. Impulsively, she moved to it. She lifted the receiver and coolly dialled. Her balloon of anticipation was promptly deflated by the engaged signal from the other end. She hung up impatiently and began the pacing again. She gave herself five minutes; but it was a great effort. Then she dialled again. This time his voice came on the line.

'Hello, darling,' she said. 'It's Dolores—remember?'

'Dolores, darling.' After the initial surprise Spencer's voice turned syrupy. 'As if you didn't know you're the one girl I never can get out of my mind.' There was amused banter in his tone, but she knew he was crazy about her, all right.

'Stop hamming it up and listen,' Dolores said. 'I've a proposition you may be interested in.'

'That's my baby,' Spencer said.

'Can you come round now and talk?'

'For you, any time. But what's so mysterious about it? What's behind that seductive veil your voice is wearing?'

'A little job I think you could handle,' Dolores said. 'An easy little job with a lot of loot attached.'

'Sounds up my dark alley,' Spencer said. He made kissing sounds into the telephone. 'Darling, put the kettle on, I'm on my way.'

CHAPTER THIRTEEN

The doorbell of 221b Harley Street shrilled and Miss Frayle jerked up and glanced at the diary on the desk.

Of course, it was Mr. Reynolds. She remembered the telephone call that morning. She looked at the clock. Five minutes to three. He was early and impatient, she added to herself, as the bell rang again.

She went into the hall and opened the front door.

'Good afternoon,' the visitor said brusquely. 'Dr. Morelle is expecting me. I'm Mr. Reynolds.'

Miss Frayle eyed him through her horn-rims with faint curiosity. 'Oh, yes,' she said. 'Please come in.'

He followed her to Dr. Morelle's consulting room, where the tall, lean figure came towards him, as Miss Frayle went out, closing the door quietly behind him.

The visitor was a big man, he had big-business tycoon written all over him. Dr. Morelle observed his clothes were obviously Saville Row, but the jacket of the dark lounge suit he was wearing appeared a trifle oversize. He had lost a little weight, and fairly recently.

It did not need the drawn, haunted look on his face, the eyes red-rimmed as though from lack of sleep, which moved nervously from side to side, the lines of premature age that etched his features, to inform Dr. Morelle that here was a human being tormented and distracted by some dark fear. He twisted his hat in his well-kept hands.

'It was very kind of you to make this appointment at such

short notice, Dr. Morelle,' he said. He had a husky voice, as if his throat was parched. He cleared his throat. 'I was most anxious to see you.'

'You mentioned Inspector Hood on the telephone?' Dr. Morelle said, regarding the other enigmatically. 'Since he is a friend of mine and I received the impression that the matter about which you wished to consult me appeared urgent, it was not unnatural I should see you. Appointments were made for men, not men for appointments.'

He offered Reynolds a cigarette from his thin gold case, but the man who sat facing him appeared in no shape to enjoy a smoke. He declined with a shake of his head and a muttered thanks. Dr. Morelle selected a Le Sphinx and lit it before he spoke again.

'What is it,' he said, 'brings you to me so urgently?'

'Blackmail.' The word was hissed out with all the contempt and anguish of which Reynolds was capable. 'I'm being black-mailed, and it's driving me insane.'

'But surely,' Dr. Morelle said calmly, 'that is a case for the police?'

'Inspector Hood sent me to you, because of the special circumstances. He told me that he could do nothing. He advised me to discuss the matter with you. Something drastic has got to be done, or—I've had it.'

Dr. Morelle raised an eyebrow. His understanding and long experience of the criminal mind and the minds of the criminal's victim had long innured him against being emotionally affected by the recounting of a personal tragedy. That evil stalked the world, none knew better than he; that innocent, or not-so-inno-cent, human beings suffered misery and terror, was a natural consequence. In order to alleviate suffering one had to remain unmoved by it, and concentrate on removing the cause.

'I fail to see,' he said quietly, 'how I can take a matter of such seriousness out of the hands of the police. In Inspector Hood you could have no better police officer to handle your case. Discreet and understanding.'

Reynolds nodded. 'I know,' he said slowly. 'But he wanted to know too much. He said he would require as much detail as I could give him.'

'Naturally,' Dr. Morelle said.

'I just couldn't give it him.' He shifted restlessly in his chair. 'And another reason I daren't go into Court. Even under the protection of Mr. X.' He leaned forward, his knuckles white as his hands gripped his hat brim. 'I've got to get myself out of this quietly.'

'Your identity wouldn't be revealed if you gave evidence,' Dr. Morelle said, 'as indeed you would have to do, otherwise the police couldn't prosecute.'

'I know. Not to the newspapers, but my wife, friends, business associates would know. That mustn't happen.'

'A woman is blackmailing you?'

Reynolds nodded and chewed at his lower lip. Dr. Morelle dragged at his cigarette silently. He was considering how he could possibly help the unfortunate wretch before him. Unless he cooperated to a much greater extent than he appeared willing to do, no one could help him.

'Have you been paying her long?'

'Several months. Months of hell.' Reynolds looked up from his trance-like stare at Dr. Morelle's fitted Wilton carpet. 'Her demands are getting more frequent, and each time I pay, it is more than the time before.'

'It's the method a woman usually adopts,' Dr. Morelle said. 'A man is less anxious to aggravate the source of his supply into taking desperate action.'

'There must be some way of dealing with her, Dr. Morelle,' the other mouthed in a desperate whisper. 'There must be. I'm at the end of my tether. I tell you, I can't take any more.'

'Have you given Inspector Hood her name?'

'No, I've told no one. I was too scared. Too scared that if I told him, he would have got to work on her, and she would have taken her revenge. Beneath the surface of her beauty and charm, she's murderously tough. She knows the position I'm in, and she'd set out to ruin me, just for the sheer hell of it.' His head suddenly drooped and he put his hands up covering his face. 'I think I could use a cigarette,' he said.

He took a Le Sphinx in fingers that shook so that he almost dropped it. Dr. Morelle had to light it for him.

'You won't get anywhere by becoming hysterical,' Dr. Morelle said. 'This is where you have to call not only upon all your reserves of moral courage, but upon your ingenuity. You are a successful businessman not lacking in common sense, I have no doubt. If I'm going to be in a position to help you at all, you must realize at once that you must be utterly frank with me. Spare me no details, however sordid.' The corners of his mouth were touched with a faint smile. 'I fancy it is unlikely that you will succeed in shocking my susceptibilities. I am a doctor, a doctor of the mind, if you like; I cannot effect a cure without a diagnosis. I cannot make a diagnosis without knowing all the symptoms.'

He studied the end of his cigarette reflectively, then said:

'Though as it is popularly supposed the female of the species may be more deadly than the male, a woman blackmailer is almost invariably less dangerous than a man. The reason being that sooner or later a woman allows her greed to overcome itself. This woman who is menacing you may be arriving at such a climax in her calculations. I shall be the better able to consider the possibilities when you have given me all the facts. She may provide us with a loophole through which we can successfully curtail her activities, without recourse to the criminal courts.'

Already there was a tinge of colour in Reynold's grey, sunken face. 'You will help me then, Dr. Morelle?' he said, his eyes gleaming with hope.

'If, as I must insist, you will first help me. Even then I can't at this stage make any solemn promise to rescue you from your predicament. I will promise to do the utmost in my power.' His gaze flicked over Reynolds, and thought he detected in his expression the sagging of hope. He sighed inwardly. The man had come expecting him to promise a miracle. And high as he undoubtedly held himself in his own opinion, even Dr. Morelle drew the line at being able to perform miracles.

'I shall require,' he said, 'this creature's name and address, every detail about her, whether you think they are relevant or not. The sums you've been paying her, for instance. The method she adopts to collect the money. What she has threatened to do if you refuse to pay. And so forth.'

Reynolds hesitated for a long moment, and Dr. Morelle, reading his thoughts as if they were written before him on a printed page, was aware that this was going to prove no easy matter. It flashed through his mind that he would not be surprised if he never saw the man again.

Finally, Reynolds looked up and began to talk in guarded staccato sentences which had to be forced from his lips by Dr. Morelle's subtle probing. The other was still inhibited by dread and panic from confiding in him as much as Dr. Morelle knew he could. Patiently and subtly as he dealt with him, and accepting that he had certainly achieved some progress, it was also obvious to him that Reynolds was not yet prepared to yield him his complete and utter confidence.

Dr. Morelle could only hope that the wretched, desperate creature would not leave it too late, before realizing where and nowhere else lay his ultimate salvation. 'When do you expect her next demand?' Dr. Morelle asked him.

'I don't know,' Reynolds said, after some hesitation. 'Not yet, surely. I last paid her only two or three weeks ago.'

'How much?'

'Er—three-fifty pounds.'

'As soon as she contacts you again, inform me,' Dr. Morelle urged him. 'Don't attempt to deal with her. Remain non-committal, whatever her threats.'

The other promised to obey instructions, and leaving an address and telephone number, he got slowly to his feet and Miss Frayle showed him out. She watched him make his way along Harley Street, until he hailed a passing taxicab and was driven away.

Dr. Morelle had lit another Le Sphinx and was considering the notes he had made of his interview with Reynolds.

The woman's name and address.

The fact that she first of all telephoned Reynolds either at his business office, or his flat in Bruton Street.

She was discreet on the telephone; she usually suggested she had a little business deal in which she knew he would be interested.

He would bring the required money to her flat. In five-pound notes.

That appeared to be the *modus operandi.*

Reynolds' wife entertained social aspirations; his colleagues on the board of his firm were straitlaced and possessed of high moral principles. It was an old established firm.

Reynolds had omitted to describe what business it was engaged in.

Dr. Morelle's eyes were slits against the smoke from his Le Sphinx. It was not difficult to appreciate the poor devil's nerve-wracking dilemma; but how did he expect that the tangled skein of deceit and lies in which by his own weakness and folly he was involved might be unravelled, if he wouldn't show strength of purpose now? His proper course, Dr. Morelle considered, was to provide the police with every possible opportunity to bring her vile career to a sharp close. At the least, he should face her menacing demands with the advice that she could proceed with her threats for what good it would do her. Dr. Morelle had no doubt in his mind what her reaction would be. She would cast about for another, more supine source of income.

What it amounted to, Dr. Morelle concluded, was that Inspector Hood had passed Reynolds over to him because he himself could get no cooperation. He had at any rate succeeded in obtaining the man's cooperation up to a point, but he still refused to provide him with sufficient material with which to enable him to force the blackmailer to relinquish her lucrative victim.

Miss Frayle returned to the consulting room as the telephone rang. He stubbed out his cigarette as Miss Frayle, her glasses slightly tilted on her nose, and behind them her eyes glowing, turned to him. She held one hand over the telephone mouthpiece, and spoke in a whisper. 'It's Mr. Gale.'

'What does he want, Miss Frayle?' Dr. Morelle said a trifle peevishly. His mind was locked with the dilemma of the individual who had just left him.

'Mr. Edwin Gale. You remember, you met him on the plane.'

'I recall him with perfect clarity, Miss Frayle. I merely required to know what he wants.'

'He's invited us to a party the evening after tomorrow,' she said. 'At his flat in Park Lane.'

There was no mistaking the enthusiasm in her tone. Dr. Morelle was frowning abstractedly at the notes he had made concerning Reynolds. His thoughts remained concentrated on the deadly situation which the other had brought to him, so that the undercurrent of excitement that had been generated by Miss Frayle answering the telephone made little impact on him. He was, nevertheless, conscious of it.

'Have I an engagement for that evening?' he said to Miss Frayle absently, and still without looking at her.

'No,' she said promptly. 'We're both free, Dr. Morelle.'

Dr. Morelle turned to regard her levelly. 'I see,' he said. 'In that case—'

But before he could finish it, Miss Frayle, all smiles of delighted anticipation (it was not often she got the opportunity of being taken to a small party by Dr. Morelle), had pushed the telephone receiver into his hand.

CHAPTER FOURTEEN

Edwin Gale left his guests and put down his drink, and hurried to the door, his heart thumping against his ribs, his stomach curiously hollow.

It was really no surprise to him that he should feel both jittery and elated at one and the same moment, for he was sure the moment heralded the introduction of the new chump. Dolores had telephoned him that morning to confirm that everything was laid on. Now it was up to him.

He opened the door, his glance ranging immediately over Dolores, the enticing central figure of the waiting trio. Any other time she would have been the exclusive focus of his attention, but now his eyes darted to the taller of the two men accompanying her; a slightly stooping, middle-aged figure with thin, Abe Lincoln-like features. Dolores introduced him as Jonathan Lang. The other man was medium height and slim, with blond wavy hair and a smallish, feminine nose. His name was Vere Spencer.

'Hallo, Edwin,' Dolores greeted him in the same lazy, seductive tones that sent his blood pressure up. 'Hope we're not too terribly late and all that.'

'Come on in,' Gale said, stepping aside. 'There're still people to come after you.'

Gale took them into the room with the sun-bronzed curtains drawn back from the windows that overlooked Park Lane, and introduced them to the handful of guests who had already arrived and were sorting themselves out over the drinks. They were an innocuous crowd, all right, he had taken care of that. Their purpose was simply to provide a backdrop for the play-acting that was to take place.

As he got himself a drink from the silver tray on the long, low table, Gale was able to get his first good look at Lang. He did not possess the genial demeanour and open countenance typical of the average wealthy, globe-trotting American. In spite of the Mediterranean pale tan he looked as if he'd been shut up in a museum all his life. His thin face and high forehead, topped by sleek dark hair, gave him the appearance of a European intellectual. Only the cigar he was smoking gave any hint that he was well-heeled.

And that was the main thing. Plus the odds that he wasn't as brainy as he looked. Gale didn't let that possibility upset him. He was confident the job he had to show Jonathan Lang would convince any expert by its authenticity. And Lang might be a keen collector, but Gale was sure he was no expert.

The party began to get underway; and Edwin Gale noticed with a possessive thrill how very quickly Dolores had become the pivot around which the small cluster of men and women, with their clinking glasses and cigarettes, drifted, chatting and laughing with each other.

Presently Gale sized up the situation as he exchanged one or two significant glances with Dolores. Everyone seemed to be enjoying the drinks and smokes that came for free; they wouldn't notice if their host faded briefly from the scene with one of the guests. So, in as unobtrusive manner as possible, he drew Jonathan Lang to one side. He lured him to the end of the windows, which were open to the cool breeze that stole in from Hyde Park. Down below the sleek cars sped in a never-ending stream, the buses rumbled, the taxis dodged their way; the lights of London's evening began to show here and there against the gathering dusk. Gale let the American make a few comparisons about Rome and London, and drew him out about his forthcoming trip homewards.

'So glad you were able to get along, Mr. Lang,' Gale said.

'You must have many engagements during your short stay in London, so I'm particularly indebted to our mutual friend Miss Dolores del Robia for bringing us together.'

'I guess the pleasure's all mine,' Lang said conventionally, taking his cigar from between his long teeth. He spoke with a soft drawl. 'When Dolores explained you and I had a mutual interest, I was most anxious to meet you.' He was eyeing Gale with a faintly quizzical expression. 'I guess she's told you my especial interest?' He put his cigar back between his teeth, and gave a vague little wave of the hand. 'Just a hobby, but I kind of take it serious.'

Gale switched on his understanding smile, his greyish-blue eyes sparkled with the friendliness of one man to another who shared a common cause. It was old hat to him, he could go through the motions in his sleep.

'And why not?' he said. 'It can be a very profitable hobby.' He put down his glass and murmured something about the beauty of the scene below. 'You must have accumulated some rare examples in your travels,' he said, as if recalling what they'd been talking about before. 'Some pretty precious first editions tucked away in places in the world.' He chuckled, and looked self-consciously complacent. 'They're not all in museums.'

'I guess not,' Lang said.

'For instance,' Gale said, 'I wonder if you've seen anything like the little sensation I came across in Spain?' He gave it just the right casualness with the underplay of an addict's serious-mindedness.

'Dolores hinted you'd got something pretty nice around,' the American said. He lowered his voice. 'I only got it from her in a casual way, Dolores is not much of a bookworm. The extrovert type, I guess.' He smiled. 'She said something about it being some logbook of one of the voyages of Christopher Columbus.'

Gale nodded with an air of proud simplicity. 'Written in his own hand in fourteen-ninety-two. It concerns his trips to the Caribbees, with his beloved *Santa Maria*, and a couple of cara-vels, the *Pinta* and the *Niña*. You may remember the trouble he had with his crews; how the variations of the magnetic needle scared the pants off them.' The stuff rattled off his tongue as glib as if he really knew what he was talking about. He didn't, of course, but he had mugged it up; and it was the way he put it over made him sound convincing.

The glow that crept beneath Lang's tanned cheekbones warmed Gale's heart. The job was a pushover. He had never had it so good. But he had to be careful. He mustn't let his confidence lead him into a slip. It had been no plan of his to close the deal there and then. Too risky. It would give Lang too much time to mull over the thing before he took off for New York. And if there was a flaw in that work of art, he might detect it, and thus bring Gale's dreams crashing into the dust.

Lang was finishing his drink and looking idly at the other guests. Gale said: 'If you'd like to take a look-see, this is an excellent opportunity.'

'Please lead me to it,' Lang said.

Gale guided him unobtrusively out of the room, as if he might be showing him the bathroom. Out of the corner of his eye, he saw Dolores, dark and gorgeous, laughing with the blond chap and a little circle of the others round her. Her throat was firm and pale bronze against the blackness of her rippling hair. At the end of the short passage he opened a door, and followed Lang into the small, book-lined study. Here there was a desk, a couple of leather easy chairs, a leather-topped table under the window. An air of masculine opulence about it all.

Lang glanced around in admiration as Gale closed the door. Gale was congratulating himself that every little thing was going to schedule. He was getting the principal business of the evening over before Dr. Morelle and Miss Frayle arrived. When he had suggested the invitation, he had intentionally given Dr. Morelle and Miss Frayle a time which he had estimated would ensure him half an hour with Lang after Dolores had brought him along. He didn't expect Dr. Morelle and Miss Frayle for a quarter of an hour yet. Time enough.

He crossed to the desk and switched on the angle-lamp.

'A quiet drink?' he said, with a nod towards the drinks cupboard in the corner of the wall. 'Whisky?'

'Thanks,' the other shook his head, 'but I left one in the other room.'

Gale unlocked a middle drawer in the writing desk. He felt inside, and brought out a small, battered-looking, leather-covered volume. A musty smell rose from it and the pages creaked as he flipped through them, mottled and yellowed, in the warm glow of the reading lamp.

Lang reached out eagerly and Gale let him take it. He handled it with obvious affection. He turned back the pages to examine the faded spidery writing and the strange figures which each page contained. With the other's eyes riveted on it, Gale talked a little, adding colour and authenticity to the precious item.

Lang nodded, glancing up with an absent look in his eyes.

'Never seen or heard of anything like this,' he said. 'It's magnificent—' He broke off, hesitated, then went on diffidently. 'It'd be the greatest to take home.' His eyes were fixed on Gale like those of a trusting puppy.

J.K. was right, Edwin Gale told himself. It really was like taking candy from a kid. 'Undoubtedly fabulous historical value,' he said. After a suitable pause: 'When are you planning to leave for the States?'

'Just a week today.'

'I was thinking, if you're really interested in it, and since you are a friend of Dolores—'

'Interested? You can say that again. I'm nuts for it. If you want to sell—' He broke off and frowned. 'Why? What's it got to do when I take off from here? If you know your mind, I can clinch a deal here and now.'

Gale hesitated, he looked a little perturbed. 'The fact is— look, I've had another offer for it, and—'

'You have?' Lang interrupted him anxiously. 'What's the figure?'

Gale rasped his plump chin with a thoughtful finger for a moment as if reluctant to talk, as if it was unfair, even unethical, to expect him to shoot his mouth, then he said softly: 'Eighteen thousand. Pounds.' He could feel his knees trembling as he spoke, although his voice sounded steady enough.

'I'll give you twenty thousand. Pounds. Right here and now.'

When he heard the other put it into words, it still took his breath away, though this was the way he'd meant it to go; twenty thousand pounds, he had to cover up by frowning and turning to look out of the window, where he thought the view of the leafy trees between Park Lane and Hyde Park had never looked so appealing. There was a singing noise in his ears. His knees were trembling, so that he thought the other couldn't fail to see them, and he moved round behind the writing desk, so as to hide his legs.

'I'm sorry if I appear a little uncooperative, Mr. Lang,' he said, a little pompously. 'I assure you that is not my intention, but the man who made me the offer is away at the moment. Travelling abroad. I can't get in touch with him. In view of his offer, it was a firm offer, I really think I must explain the position to him first. I'm sure you understand?'

His greyish-blue eyes were full of good fellowship and appeal for sympathy in his difficult circumstances.

'Sure,' the other said. But Edwin Gale saw with satisfaction the disappointment on his face. 'When does he get back?'

'Not until the end of next week, I'm afraid,' Gale said. He put on a sudden thoughtfully magnanimous expression. 'What I will do tomorrow,' he said, 'is try and find out where he is. Nice, I somehow think. Or was it Cannes? If I can find him, I'll rush him a cable, or get him on the phone.'

Lang's thin face which had gone hollow under his cheek-bones, filled out again. 'That's really great of you. I do appreciate that.' Lang smiled at him, overflowing with warm gratitude. 'I'll leave it to you to try and fix it my way.'

Gale murmured a response, as if he would move heaven and earth to persuade this character over there in Nice—or was it Cannes?—not to give him that eighteen thousand for the relic. He could feel Lang's envious eyes on it, as he returned the musty, mildewy, leather volume to the desk drawer and turned the key.

CHAPTER FIFTEEN

Miss Frayle's wide, innocent eyes sparkled behind her horn-rimmed spectacles as she glanced round the luxuriously furnished room. Her attention almost immediately fastened on one particular figure. A tall, curvaceous figure. A dramatic-looking young woman with jet black hair and dark eyes.

Miss Frayle glanced at Dr. Morelle as Gale introduced them to his guests. Thank goodness, she thought, Dr. Morelle didn't look as if he was too bored. On their way to Park Lane he had sat broodingly at the wheel of the Duesenberg from the time they had left Harley Street. He had hardly spoken a word, and she had anxiously wondered if at the last minute he would have preferred to change his mind and spend the evening in his laboratory instead.

She hoped he wasn't going to ruin her evening by appearing irritable and moody. On the other hand, she had realized he might have just been deep in thought about some problem, and as soon as they were among people his attitude would change. She was particularly concerned to observe him as Gale proudly introduced him, anxious to impress his guests with the arrival of such a famous figure.

Now, Dr. Morelle's withdrawn expression seemed to be melting a little, and Miss Frayle could not help noticing how he seemed to brighten when he was introduced to the strikingly attractive woman who had caught her attention when they had first arrived. Dolores del Robia. And suppressing a vague pang, Miss Frayle studied the glamorous creature more closely, and came to the conclusion that she was just another of those women who flaunted their sex appeal at any and every male in the hope that it would produce some material reward from someone. Shooting off a quiverful of arrows with the idea that one must score a bull's-eye, was how she mentally described it.

Determined to enjoy the party, she deliberately turned her back on Dr. Morelle and the flashing-eyed, dark woman in her low-cut dress, and encouraged by the glass of sherry Edwin Gale had put into her hand, entered animatedly into the light conversation going on around her. The room became warm and heavy with cigarette smoke and perfume. The clink of glasses and the murmur of voices, frequently punctuated by laughter.

Miss Frayle felt she was really having a good time, chatting with half-a-dozen different people, including a nice American whom Edwin Gale had brought over to her. And there was a good-looking young man with a fascinating nose she'd had a brief snatch of conversation with. Only he'd disappeared afterwards and she hadn't seen him again. It was not until Dr. Morelle, whom she was sure was not sharing her enjoyment of the party, came to her and explained he was leaving, that she realized that the evening had gone.

Smiling his faintly sardonic smile, Dr. Morelle told her that as she was obviously entertained, there was no reason for her to accompany him, but there was work requiring his attention in the laboratory.

Dr. Morelle took his leave a few minutes later, and Miss Frayle settled down to continue her conversation with the group which included Gale and the American, whose name she learned was Lang. She caught a glimpse of the blond man again, exchanging a word with the dark beauty. He hadn't left as she'd imagined. She thought he was helping himself very liberally to the whisky, when she realized that there were signs of the party breaking up. Mr. Lang, the American, made his excuses and went, and Miss Frayle noticed that he had a moment's earnest conversation with Gale before he left with the dark, young woman, who made her extravagant farewells and who was accompanied by the blond young man.

Reluctant as she was to leave the warm, friendly party atmosphere, Miss Frayle knew it was time to go, too, and a little later she was bidding Edwin Gale goodbye.

It was as she stepped out of the lift on the ground floor, that Miss Frayle suddenly realized with concern that in the excitement of thanking Edwin Gale for the wonderful party, she had left her handbag behind. She hurried back to the flat.

Hesitantly she pressed the doorbell of the flat, hoping that Mr. Gale wouldn't think her too much of a nuisance. But when he opened the door she was taken aback to find him agitated, his eyes held a look of utter desperation and his face was drawn.

'What is it?' he said, as if he hadn't recognized her.

'I'm so sorry,' she said, 'but my handbag. I think I must have left it behind. So foolish of me—'

'Come in. Come in then, Miss Frayle,' he said, his manner jumpy, his voice irritable and rasping.

She saw her handbag at the back of one of the gilt chairs, over by the sun-bronzed curtains, where she must have absent-mindedly put it down in order to cope with her glass of sherry. She picked it up and turned to Edwin Gale, smiling her thankfulness. But his appearance was so changed that her smile vanished.

'Is—is something wrong?' she said.

'Something pretty shocking has happened,' he said, smoothing his features with a shaky hand.

'Whatever is it?' Miss Frayle said. 'Is there anything I can do to help? You look quite ill.'

'It was a priceless antique, a logbook, in fact, used by Christopher Columbus.' He suddenly found himself glad to tell someone about it. The shock when he realized it had gone was beginning to wear off, and he wanted to talk about it. 'I showed it to Mr. Lang who—who's interested in that sort of thing, and then I returned the book to my desk. And—and now it's gone.'

She stared at him. 'You mean that someone—here, at the party—has stolen it?'

'I don't know—I don't know what to think.'

He slumped into a chair, staring dejectedly in front of him. Miss Frayle bit her lower lip in anxious sympathy. If only Dr. Morelle had been there. He would know what to do. He would have known how to act. She put her thoughts into words.

'Why don't you let Dr. Morelle know?' He started to shake his head, but she went on enthusiastically. 'He will advise you what to do,' she said. He stood up as if to say something to her, but she smiled at him as if he were a child who'd lost his favourite toy. 'Don't you worry, Mr. Gale. Leave all the worrying to Dr. Morelle. No, don't say a word. I'll make an appointment for you and ring you first thing in the morning.'

Gale looked at her with his mouth half-open. His shoulders sagged. 'It—it's very good of you,' he said.

Miss Frayle smiled at him with supreme confidence. 'Dr. Morelle will have it back for you in no time,' she said.

CHAPTER SIXTEEN

Dolores splashed some soda water into Vere Spencer's whisky glass. She refilled her own glass, watching Spencer out of the corner of her eye. He was comfortably settled on the settee, relaxed over the leather-tattered volume with its musty smell.

'Don't know much about these things, but it looks the real McCoy to me. I can't fault it.' He took his drink and raised it, his eyes greedy. 'Here's to you and me and Christopher Columbus.'

They drank.

He opened his cigarette case and she took a cigarette. He held his lighter to it and then lit his own. Lazily he exhaled a trail of smoke.

'And,' he said, smiling at her fondly, 'what other bright ideas are nesting in that pretty head, darling? What's the next step on the way to the jackpot?'

'How we deal with Lang,' she said thoughtfully over the rim of her glass, 'without making him damned nosey about Edwin Gale.'

'Obvious, we can't do anything about it here, in London,' Spencer said. 'We'll have to wait till he's back in the States, and then go after him. We'll have to clinch the deal over there.'

Dolores nodded. She took a long drink at her gin.

'That's the way I see it. If we don't want to raise his suspicions. If we attempt to try it on before he leaves, he'll get on to Gale, pronto.'

'One consolation,' Spencer said. 'We know he'll never go to the cops to yell about his loss. He'll be too scared they might find out it's a faked job.'

'I'm not worried about that,' Dolores said. 'But whipping over to New York is a different caper. That'll need money.'

'Only one of us need make the trip,' Vere Spencer said. 'No point paying two fares when it should only need one to pull off the deal.'

Dolores' eyes had slitted so that their glitter was almost hidden by the thick, mascarad lashes, but her expression remained serene. She smiled. 'And I suppose you see yourself in the role of globe-trotting salesman, darling?'

Spencer finished his drink and automatically passed his glass back to her. He was beginning to mellow a bit now. His nerves had been stretched to their limit while he'd been engaged on swiping that precious logbook thing out of Edwin Gale's writing desk.

'Not necessarily,' he said easily. 'Depends which one of us would best handle the deal. From where I'm sitting, I'd say it's you. But we can decide that later. Let's rustle up the cash for the trip first.'

'Huh-huh,' she said. 'Let's do that. It doesn't grow in window boxes.'

Dolores moved over to the low chest where the decanters and bottles and glasses gleamed. She was generous with the whisky and mean with the soda-syphon. Certainly she wasn't going to trust that flat, leather-covered job out of her sight. The nicer she was towards Spencer and the more generous with the drink, the easier her task would be to restrain him from hanging on to it, if that was his idea.

She had a feeling that was his idea. She wouldn't put it beyond him to try something funny, when his brain began working and he began thinking things, he could even try to double-cross her, if the opportunity arose.

She sat down beside him again, and he took the glass and then he suddenly leaned over, put his arms around her, and kissed her on the mouth. She let him get on with it, and returned his kisses, deciding that it suited her that way.

'You're my favourite girl, Dolores,' he said, thickly.

Her eyes were mocking, her voice teasing.

'Just for the moment,' she said.

'For all time,' he said. 'Always have been.'

Dolores pushed him away. 'Well, sit up, darling,' she said, 'and act like you respect me.' She handed him his drink. 'Here, your drink's going cold.'

She got up, and while the other watched her lasciviously, she put her empty glass with the decanters. 'We haven't a lot of time to work out how to raise the cash,' she said. 'I suggest you go home now, darling, and get yourself some sleep. Tomorrow maybe we can pool our ideas.'

He caught the tone of dismissal and scowled. This wasn't how he'd expected the evening would end. He felt like celebrating, and there was no one he wanted to celebrate with more than her.

Casually she picked up the object of their joint enterprise and took it to the little Georgian bureau in the corner. She unlocked a drawer and slid it inside. Then looked across and smiled at him, as she turned the key. She dropped the key into a silver cigarette box, pushed the cigarettes back over it, and snapped the heavy lid shut.

Spencer was watching her, but he didn't smile back.

'I took it for granted,' he said slowly, 'you'd want me to keep it in safekeeping. I mean, supposing Gale comes snooping around here?'

'Save yourself the worry about that, darling. I can take care of him.' She came over to him and snuggled in his arms. 'Besides,' she said, her mouth against his, 'think how tragic it would be if you lost it on your way home.'

He ran his hands over her and kissed her. 'You're insufferable,' he said thickly, and kissed her again.

After he'd gone, she began to get ready to go to bed. She slipped into a dressing gown of severe, almost masculine cut, and sat staring at her reflection in the dressing table mirror. She picked up Vere Spencer's white silk scarf from the floor where it had fallen earlier on, and hung it over a chair back. She couldn't remember whether he had worn it that evening when he'd called to pick her up to take her along to Curzon's Hotel, where they were meeting Lang, before going on to the party, or whether he had left it on some previous visit. Spencer was always leaving things at her flat. She knew he did it deliberately, to give him the idea that their relationship was really intimate.

She frowned at her face in the mirror and went into the sitting room, got herself another drink and a cigarette, and began pacing up and down.

Spencer had done a good job, and she was sure Gale had no suspicion of their complicity. So far they were safe enough. But what about the rest of it? Her first intention had been to share the proceeds with Spencer. But now she had her doubts about the necessity of sticking to their agreement.

She glanced at the bureau in the corner, and her eyes took on a greedy expression.

Spencer had been right about doing nothing while Lang was in London. There was no alternative to going to America after Lang and negotiating the sale there. But Spencer's idea at first that they should both go, that wasn't so good. And she knew that when the time came and she tried to make the trip herself, without him, he would take it badly. Especially as he would by then have helped her to finance the trip.

He'd never trust her to play it straight once she got to America. Any more than she'd trust him. She wouldn't even trust him in London if he'd got the phoney relic in his claws.

Supposing she'd let him take it, and he could somehow raise the cash to get him to the U.S.? Wasn't it likely that without a word to her, he'd slip over immediately and await Lang's arrival?

The more she thought about this angle, the more certain it seemed a potential reality. If that idea did occur to him—and it might, as easily as it had occurred to her—then he wouldn't stop at mere charm and persuasion in order to get the property back. Where he'd stolen it once, he could steal it again.

She stubbed out her cigarette and finished the drink, her eyes narrow, her thoughts twisting round her brain like snakes.

If Spencer intended to double-cross her, then by acting first she was only protecting herself and her own interests, she was telling herself. She would have to move fast.

She was confident if she got to New York and awaited Lang's arrival she would have no difficulty in putting over the deal. The twenty thousand would be hers. All of it. She would have to concoct a plausible story to satisfy him, but there would be time enough to dream up something when she got there. The important thing was to get there, with enough money in hand to allow her to put up with the right kind of front. A smart New York hotel and all the rest of it. That meant money and plenty of it. Now.

Where could she get the amount?

Quickly?

Her dark gaze lingered on the telephone.

There was only one source that could supply her with what she wanted, and fast.

She was smiling to herself.

It was not a very nice smile. She wasn't smiling with her eyes.

She picked up the receiver with a swift movement and began dialling.

She was still smiling.

CHAPTER SEVENTEEN

Edwin Gale's mingled apprehension and anxiety was not only due to the staggering knowledge that the theft had happened under his nose, but also to the fact that, without proper consideration of the consequences, he had allowed himself to be persuaded by Miss Frayle into agreeing to consult Dr. Morelle about it.

After a sleep-banished night, during which he had fully realized the folly and danger of bringing Dr. Morelle on to the scene, he was still unable to think of a way of backing out of the visit to Harley Street, without, he feared, appearing suspiciously evasive, not only in Miss Frayle's eyes, but also to Dr. Morelle.

There was nothing he could do, it seemed, but go through with it and hope he could retrieve the situation speedily without Dr. Morelle's intervention.

The telephone rang and he glanced at his watch, and cursed softly to himself.

He picked up the instrument reluctantly.

'Mr. Gale? Oh, good morning. Miss Frayle here. Dr. Morelle says he will be pleased to see you if you'd care to call at Harley Street at eleven-thirty this morning.'

Gale could do nothing but lie that he would be glad to come along. After he had hung up, he decided grimly that he was wearing his nerves to a frazzle unnecessarily. He even decided that it would make a most convincing impression upon Lang, when the stolen item was recovered and he could go through with the deal after all. To be able to say that he had called in the great Dr. Morelle himself to ensure the safe return of the relic would sound pretty good.

And so he took a taxi to Harley Street in a much more relaxed frame of mind. He wondered what line Dr. Morelle would adopt, and what sort of information he would be asked for. No doubt he would be expected to give the minutest details about the object of the theft, and he would have to watch out not to give away the show to that astute mind with which he had already made some acquaintance.

A little later he was in Dr. Morelle's study, and any fears he may have felt had very largely evaporated before the sympathetic attention with which Miss Frayle received him. While over coffee and an inevitable Le Sphinx, Dr. Morelle's attitude quickly reassured Gale that so long as he was careful, he would have little to worry about.

'You showed the relic to Mr. Lang during the party, just before I arrived? This was in your study. Afterwards you locked it away in a drawer of your desk and did not discover its loss until everyone had gone.' Dr. Morelle paused and contemplated the tip of his cigarette. 'What made you unlock the drawer again? Had you suspicions of anyone?'

Edwin Gale shook his head. He explained, with complete truth, that there had been no specific reason for his unlocking the drawer for another view of the prize which he had only shortly before left there, safe.

He felt that his story sounded convincing enough. It should have done. It was largely true. When he'd seen that drawer gaping up at him, empty, he had thought he was going out of his mind.

Dr. Morelle stared levelly at Gale. 'Who among your guests besides Lang, of course, knew that you had such a valuable item in your flat?'

Gale hesitated for a moment. This was where a trap opened before him. Dolores was the only one of whom he was sure, but he was reluctant to mention her. If Dr. Morelle questioned her, she might let something slip about their business arrangement.

He didn't want Dr. Morelle to know about a little thing like that. Or she might be panicked into saying something which could give the whole show away. On the other hand, wouldn't Dr. Morelle want to know how he had made Lang's acquaintance? He would have to tip off Dolores about all this. As these thoughts flashed through his mind, so did an answer to Dr. Morelle's question.

'I wouldn't say that I can pick out any particular one as a likely suspect,' he said, trying his best not to sound evasive. 'I doubt if anyone there had an inkling of the deal I was discussing with Lang. Unless, of course, he himself had mentioned something about it to someone.'

Dr. Morelle's expression gave no hint of what he was thinking. The question Gale was afraid he would ask, he didn't. 'Apart from him,' he said, 'were your guests close friends?'

'I wouldn't say close friends,' Gale said. 'I know them pretty well. Business. Parties. And so on. But I'd never met Vere Spencer before.'

'How did he come to be invited?'

'He came with Miss del Robia and Lang.'

'Did you happen to notice if he was missing at any time during the party?'

'I can't say I did. Apart from looking after everyone, I spent a lot of time with Lang.' Gale stroked his chin reflectively. 'Spencer may have gone to the bathroom, of course. That's just opposite the study.'

'From what we know so far,' Dr. Morelle said, 'it would seem logical to start with him. You don't know where he lives?'

'No,' Gale said.

'If he is an acquaintance of Miss del Robia or Mr. Lang, either one of them would be able to give us his address.'

He opened the door and called for Miss Frayle. When he asked her to check the telephone directory for Vere Spencer, she gave a sudden exclamation. 'That was the blond young man,' she said. 'I remember now noticing that he wasn't around. In fact, I thought he'd left. Then he appeared as the party was breaking up and went off with the dark woman and Mr. Lang.'

Dr. Morelle looked at her with hooded eyes, his expression as enigmatic as ever, but Gale rose to the implication in what she said.

'As I've said, I know nothing about him. He might be the type to get himself invited somewhere where he thinks there maybe valuables to be obtained. Not that I'm accusing him,' he said quickly. 'But if Miss Frayle happened to notice his absence there might well have been something in it.'

Miss Frayle returned a few moments later with Spencer's address. 'He's on the telephone,' she said.

Gale fidgeted and looked across at Dr. Morelle, frowning.

'What I would like to suggest,' Gale said, 'is that I would be prepared to offer something for the return of my property. Whoever the thief might be.' He hesitated and then: 'I know this isn't strictly lawful, but I'm anxious to avoid any publicity. You see, I've no wish to upset Mr. Lang, and if the police were called in, there'd be all kinds of delays and other difficulties which might spoil the deal. You will appreciate I'm most anxious to avoid this. If it should be necessary to pay up to a certain amount to keep the thing quiet, I shall be quite willing.'

'It will depend on developments,' Dr. Morelle said non-committally. A glimmer of a smile flickered across his lips. 'First, we must find the thief.'

'You can have every confidence in Dr. Morelle,' Miss Frayle said to Gale, encouragingly.

'I'm sure,' Edwin Gale said. 'I'm most grateful for your kind offer of help.' And he did his best to look like it.

'If you will leave the matter with me,' Dr. Morelle said. 'I'll give it due thought, and will be in touch with you as soon as I have decided what would be the wisest course to pursue.'

After Edwin Gale had gone, Miss Frayle returned to Dr. Morelle's study. He looked up as she came in from some notes on his desk.

'What are you going to do about it?' Miss Frayle asked.

'It might be fruitful to have a word with Miss del Robia,' he said. 'First.'

Miss Frayle's mouth fell open. 'Her?' she said. She was suddenly recalling that he had appeared more than a little intrigued by her last night at the party. 'I suppose she's very lovely,' she said, inconsequentially.

'I fail to see quite what that would have to do with my interest in her,' Dr. Morelle said. 'Except, of course, that beauty, like charity, may cover a multitude of sins.'

CHAPTER EIGHTEEN

The sun filtered through the pale curtains across the room strewn with clothes and caught one half of the rumpled bed.

Vere Spencer stirred in his sleep as an edge of light caught his face. He moaned, and then one eyelid flickered and he squinted at the window wondering why the sunshine in the room was so brilliant. He sat up cautiously, opening the other eye slowly, and focusing the silver travelling clock on the bedside table.

It was twelve thirty-seven.

He groaned again and slumped back into the pillows. He felt ghastly. His mouth felt like the bottom of a gravel pit. His head throbbed sickeningly. His stomach felt as if it would turn a triple somersault at any minute. He'd got a terrific hangover. Memory came back to him and he managed a weak grin. He'd also got that damned loot from Edwin Gale.

Memory did another surge up into his brain, and the grin faded.

He'd got the thing, but not anymore. Dolores had got it now. He smoothed his hand gingerly across his throbbing temples.

Not to worry, he told himself. Of course, Dolores had got it, she was taking care of it for them. Soon it would be converted into cash.

Twenty thousand pounds.

He got out of bed very slowly. He didn't wait to put on his dressing gown.

When he came back from the bathroom he felt a bit better, though the sunlight in the curtained bedroom made his eyes ache still. He tottered back to the bathroom and found some alkaline salts in the cupboard. He managed to mix himself a draught and get it down. It nearly made him vomit some more, but he managed to avoid doing so and staggered back to the bed, where he collapsed, groaning.

The street outside was quiet, but he could hear the rumble of traffic from the direction of the King's Road.

He'd made a night of it and no mistake. He couldn't recall where he'd got to after he'd left Dolores. Except that he'd set out for Soho. He probably never would remember where he'd started off on his spree or what other clubs, dumps, and dives he'd landed up in. He remembered the Song-and-Dance, because he'd been there plenty of times before. There was a girl in the floorshow. Only he hadn't gone home with her. It had been another little number this time. A brunette with a round face and a fringe.

That must have been his last port of call, the Song-and-Dance, even if he'd looked in there earlier. It had been bacon-and-eggs—his stomach rose up in his throat at the recollection and he fought it down again—and the last show.

All that came back to him, and so did some of what had followed. It was the earlier part of the night which was blank. He screwed up his eyes and concentrated on remembering what he could. The little, baby-faced brunette with the fringe whose ways weren't a bit babylike.

He could now vaguely remember letting himself into his own house as the dawn light streaked the sky. He didn't remember leaving the girl's flat. He didn't remember where it was located. He couldn't even remember her name. But he remembered he'd had a good time. He'd find the brunette again at the club.

His thoughts returned to the party in Park Lane.

The best pickings of his life. Twenty thousand pounds. He grinned to himself once more. That was something like a cool ten thousand each. Just as well though, he reflected sourly, that Dolores had persuaded him to leave it with her. He might have lost it last night. He certainly would have lost the thing.

His stomach turned over and he went into the bathroom again. But now he was feeling much better and he ran the bath. He gargled the sour taste out of his mouth. He felt even better when he'd shaved. He couldn't bear stubble on his round chin. He always shaved again if he had an evening date. Afterwards he went down to the kitchen to make some strong coffee. After a couple of cups, black and strong without any sugar, he felt approaching normal again. He lounged back in a chair at the table smoking a cigarette and idly stirring his third cup of coffee.

Vere Spencer began to do a little mental arithmetic. How much folding money would he need for the New York trip? Just enough for a single passage and a little over to put up a front in New York while he closed the deal with Lang. That wouldn't cost a lot. He could scrape by on, say, two hundred pounds.

But where would he lay his hands on even that relatively small amount quickly?

He suddenly checked his calculations, as he realized the line his thoughts were taking. He was thinking things out as if he were playing the lone hand. As if he was taking that blasted fake across to New York and doing the deal by himself and for himself? What about Dolores? He was sure she wasn't going to agree to his taking the trip. Not on his ownsome. He recalled that last night he'd obligingly suggested that she should make the trip.

She'd obviously got that in mind, anyway. He had certainly had the feeling that she didn't trust him.

He recalled how she'd quietly locked the damned thing away. She'd given him no hint of how or if she could raise the cash for the fare. But if she was so dead keen on chasing after Lang herself, she would have to raise it.

He lit his third cigarette and he began to think about the scene between him and Dolores at her flat. It all stood out sharp and clear in his mind. He wasn't a bit hazy about what had happened after he and Dolores had left the Park Lane flat with Lang. He recollected with a little grin that he'd been secretly amused at the knowledge that he had the very stuff on him which the

American chump would give twenty thousand pounds for and gladly, right there in his pocket all the time.

They had left Lang at Curzon's Hotel, talking their way out of his invitation to stay for eats. He had gone back with Dolores to Cheval Mews.

The flat where right now Dolores had the potential twenty thousand pounds.

Suddenly he felt sick. Only this time it was nothing to do with his hangover. He was beginning to view things in a more sinister light.

It began to occur to him that her action had been a sort of insinuation. She had wanted him to know that she'd complete control of their partnership. She was the boss.

To hell with that idea, he thought. He'd taken all the risk; now she'd got the goods. It was the wrong way round.

Resentment mingled with a grinding fear welled up inside him. He stubbed out his cigarette and at the back of his mind a question mark uncoiled itself and grew larger and larger as he considered it. Supposing she planned to double-cross him? Supposing, in fact, she knew where she could raise the cash for the New York trip and quickly? Then there could be a motive for holding on to that musty, bogus relic in the bureau drawer.

His mind increasingly ill at ease he went back upstairs and automatically began tidying up the bedroom, collecting his clothes. His daily help came in from nine o'clock till eleven every morning. She had failed to wake him for breakfast, a situation she was not altogether unaccustomed to, and had taken her departure.

After he had made his own bed, with several pauses to nurse his still aching head, and the exercise didn't help it much, he began dressing slowly. All the time his thoughts swirled more and more bitterly round inside his head.

Several hours later he had convinced himself that he knew what it was all in aid of. The double-cross.

All right, two could play at that caper. If all that had gone between them amounted to nothing just because twenty thousand was the prize, he could feel that way, too. He could forget that they'd been lovers, that she'd meant a lot to him. Even if he hadn't meant so much to her.

That was the way she wanted it, that was the way she could have it. It was a question of who struck first.

He knew her well enough to know that he'd have to watch all the angles. He'd look in on her that evening. He wouldn't rush at it. He'd have a drink or two first, because that would give him confidence and a plausible story. He'd have to convince her of the necessity for him to take over care of the prize. It would have to be something that would allay her suspicions. Something that would be a clincher. It would have to be something good.

Perhaps he'd give her a casual ring before he went along. But he'd have to work out something. He began turning over in his mind what it could be that would persuade her to unlock that bureau drawer and hand over the contents into his protection.

CHAPTER NINETEEN

It was no good, the more he turned it over in his mind, the less Edwin Gale liked the idea of allowing Dr. Morelle to have anything to do with the business.

The reaction had set in.

He had left the house in Harley Street in an optimistic mood. He had felt sure that there was in fact little chance that Dr. Morelle would succeed where he himself would fail; or if by some lucky chance he did, then there would be no reason why anything about it should come to the knowledge of the police.

He felt he could congratulate himself on having made a virtue of necessity.

But as the morning slipped into the afternoon, another thought had occurred to him. What if Dr. Morelle, if and when he should locate the item, discovered it to be a fake? He realized that this was the disastrous risk he had run in accepting Miss Frayle's offer the previous night. If the discovery of its loss hadn't gone to his head, he would never have given away to her what had happened.

Gale lunched thoughtfully at a quiet grill room in Mayfair and walked leisurely back to his flat in the afternoon sun, his mind still groping with the problem. His mood was growing more bitter, so that even the hall porter at Parkside House became an intrusion when he greeted him with a remark about the beautiful weather.

In his study he opened the drawer where the focal point of his grandiose dreams had reposed.

He scowled at the empty space.

Who had taken it?

Spencer, the blond young man who had accompanied Dolores and Lang? Certainly from Miss Frayle's observations it would seem he was the only guest whose behaviour had cast a shred of suspicion. Could he have been in the bathroom all that time? There would seem to be no reason for him to be there for more than a few minutes unless he had been taken ill. And no one of the party had been ill last night.

Supposing then, Spencer was the culprit; how had he known what the desk drawer held? How had he known of the existence of the Columbus logbook? He was a friend of Dolores. How much of a friend? Whatever their acquaintanceship, Gale could see no reason why Dolores should tell him anything, unless she had let something slip in conversation with Lang in Spencer's hearing.

All the same, there was no getting away from the fact that, if Spencer was the thief, somehow he had discovered where the swag was kept and that it was worth the taking. Did he also know it was a fake? That was a frightening thought. Then, Gale thought, if he did know it, only Dolores could have told him that. There would have been no leak from Outram, of that he was certain. If Spencer had got it and was approached by Dr. Morelle and he knew the truth about it, he might come out with the fact that it was a forgery. Edwin Gale started to sweat a little.

It was quite possible that even Dr. Morelle's astute mind might take the job as authentic. But if Spencer had learned its origin and was anxious to cover himself, it would be likely as not that he'd give the game away. And that would wash up Gale forever.

He went out of the study and wandered round the flat. He would have to know something. He couldn't content himself just hanging around doing nothing, leaving it to Dr. Morelle. He'd have to beat him to it. He'd have to get on to Dolores. If she wasn't in the know already, and his eyes glittered at the possibility that she'd tipped off Vere Spencer, she'd got to know what had happened anyway. And if she was in the clear about the whole thing, she'd know something about Spencer. She'd surely have a good idea whether he was the thief or not.

And if it wasn't Vere Spencer, who the hell else could it be?

He crossed to the telephone. He dialled her number and he heard it ringing the other end of the wire. It seemed a long time before he realized there was going to be no reply and he lowered the receiver.

He stood there, wondering where she might be. Finally, he shook off the inertia which had suddenly possessed him. There was nothing unusual in her being out. He'd just have to be patient a bit longer. Then he'd go and see her. He wouldn't ring any more. He'd just go round. Early that evening. Perhaps he'd take her to dinner somewhere quiet where they could talk. And then they could go back to the flat—his thoughts began to revolve round her dramatic face and alluring shape, and he forgot about his deadly loss for a few moments.

Presently he began to think that everything would work out after all. It was only at intervals during the rest of the day that the black cloud of bitterness and frustration engulfed him. He toyed with the idea of looking in at the Bookworm with the idea that he might pick up a clue there. But he was positive that Outram hadn't sold him up the river to anyone, and he didn't want any more people to know about the theft. Already one too many knew.

Dr. Morelle.

Soon after seven-thirty that evening he paid off his taxi and made his way to Cheval Mews. He had made the taxi stop some distance from the mews; he thought it might be more discreet not to advertise his arrival to anyone. When he reached the steps leading up to Dolores' front door, he looked up and was surprised to notice that the blue-painted door was partly open. He looked round the dreary, deserted mews, wondering if she had just slipped out. He frowned to himself, he hoped he hadn't missed her and that she wouldn't be long. Then he recollected there'd been a little pub nearby, he had passed it after he paid off the taxi. Maybe that was it. She'd gone out to get a bottle of something. He decided to go into the flat anyway, and wait if she wasn't there.

He called out quietly at the door, but there was no reply. He went in. The sitting room was empty. He called through to the bedroom, softly again, but there was no reply. He stood against the settee looking round reflectively.

He was thinking that once the business was over and the cash in the kitty, he was sure he could count on Dolores giving him a good time. Her unspoken promise once they'd brought off the sale to Lang lingered in his mind. He thought they ought to get along pretty well together.

The sudden thought of the beautiful dream slipping through his fingers if he failed to latch on to that damned fake relic brought him back to realities with a jolt. He wondered, his thoughts drifting off bitterly, what Dr. Morelle had found out, if anything. Perhaps he hadn't done anything about it after all. Perhaps he'd decided it wasn't really worthy of his attention. Then he asked himself, for the hundredth time: how was Dolores going to react when he told her the news?

He felt his angry frustration riding him again. She'd think him a fool. After the smart way she'd handled Lang for him, after she'd set the deal up for him, given it to him on a plate— and now to let this happen. Maybe she would have an idea or two, anyway; how long was she going to be?

He had done quite a bit of waiting around for her. Controlling his impatience this afternoon, and now while she'd slipped out for a drink or something, he was waiting again.

His nerves on edge, he moved across to the door to the bedroom. It was half-open. Impulsively, he pushed it wider. Her perfume filled his nostrils, as without knowing why he suddenly went in.

It was small and luxurious with a warm, pink décor. The divan bed was low and wide and covered with a pink silk spread. There was the gilt dressing table part of which he had glimpsed from the sitting room. It was topped with a glass tray filled with a miscellany of feminine aids to beauty. The wardrobe was burred walnut and stood next to the window where the partly-drawn pink curtains obscured most of the view outside. Gale's eyes were attracted to one or two items of lingerie on the foot of the bed. He thought the black filmy nightdress was the most interesting.

He started to move across the room, but he didn't get any further than the gilt dressing table. A drawer was pulled out and his attention was attracted by a bundle of glossy objects beneath some letters. They were photographs.

He picked them up. There were half a dozen prints of Dolores. She was with a man, a middle-aged man. In some of the poses she hadn't any clothes on, in some she had so little on it couldn't have mattered less.

A pain started up over Gale's right eyebrow. There was a warm feeling in his mouth. He'd bumped into this sort of thing before and hadn't batted an eyelid; but now he felt sick to the stomach. He knew now where her expensive perfume, her eye-catching clothes, and her cosy flat came from.

He hadn't given it a thought before. It just hadn't occurred to him where she might have got her money. He'd imagined there was someone, some rich admirer footing a few bills. Maybe an ex-husband coughing up some alimony.

He thought he heard a sound outside and he pushed the glossy prints back into the drawer. He noticed as he did so that the handwriting on the letters was masculine. A thought flashed through his mind. Had J.K. known about this?

He saw another door which was closed. He thought it might lead to the bathroom, and he decided to get into the bathroom. He didn't want her to suspect he had the low-down on her now. He could pretend he'd gone to the bathroom while he was waiting for her.

As he moved to the door he saw a scarf hung over the back of a chair. It was a man's scarf, white silk; and then just behind the chair, where they'd fallen was a pair of pyjama trousers. Men's pyjamas.

They were pale blue silk, just the sort, he knew, as if he could see him there, in them, that a blond slim young man like Vere Spencer would wear. As the hunch grew into a conviction that Spencer and Dolores were lovers, he heard the front door slam and he knew that Dolores was back.

He slipped out into a tiny passage. There was a door to his left which obviously opened on to the sitting room, and he turned the handle carefully and inched the door open.

CHAPTER TWENTY

Gale didn't know how he got his feelings under control. He supposed it was the opening of the front door of the flat that pulled his outraged senses together. He'd got to keep calm, he told himself. No use dashing out at her like a mad bull if he was to find out the whole truth. He'd have to play his cards carefully if he was going to take the last trick. Pretend he knew nothing, suspected nothing. Though, God knows, it required a superhuman effort. There was a throbbing pain over his right eye.

Dolores had taken him for a ride, no doubt about it. She'd flashed her lovely dark eyes at him and led him just far enough. Far enough so that she could fence him off with a promise. And all the time it was Spencer who was the lover-boy. As for him, she was simply using him to get her hands on the loot he'd put her way. She wasn't going to be satisfied with her cut. When the deal was over, she'd chuck him aside like a cigarette butt. She'd leave him right out in the cold, to whistle for his share of the deal. The throbbing over his eye was still there.

He forced his brain to simmer down. As he regained his self-control, he could see how the scheme had worked. Dolores had wised up Spencer about the precious relic and the proposed deal with Lang. It had been a simple matter to work Spencer into the party. Dolores had kept close to Lang all during the party, as if Spencer was just someone who'd come along on the spur of the moment.

Spencer, who had made the grab when he absented himself from the room. Spencer had got away with it. Gale supposed

THE MIND OF DR. MORELLE | 127

he'd that damned fake relic safely tucked away somewhere at his place. But what were they intending to do? Lie low and wait, and then try and clinch the deal with Lang just before he left for America? Or offer it back to him—at a price? He broke into a cold sweat at the thought that they might discover its worthlessness. That would blow the whole works sky-high. But no, there wasn't any reason why they should tumble to it. It had fooled Lang, who after all was something of an expert.

He dismissed the possibility as being unlikely. He'd have to try and find out their game first, and then get to know where Spencer had got the thing. His mouth was a grim line. Dolores might be a smart operator, but he would beat her at her own racket.

The pain over his eye was subsiding. He felt quite calm when he stepped silently out of the bedroom and along the passage. He was determined not to throw away the advantage he now had through careless and hysterical behaviour.

He paused at the door of the living room and looked through the crack between the door edge and the jamb. He could see only part of the room, and Dolores wasn't within his restricted view, but he could hear her moving about. He was about to push the door wide open when the telephone bell suddenly shrilled. It made him jump slightly his nerves were that on edge, but any noise he might have made was covered by the jangling bell, and Dolores' movements as she crossed the room to answer it. He stood perfectly still, listening.

'Hullo,' she said and then in that languorous voice of hers: 'Why, hullo, Vere, darling. I was just thinking about you.'

The pain spread over Gale's right temple now as he listened to her. He couldn't know she was still acting a part. It was all he could do to stand still, and his only movement was the unconscious clenching and unclenching of his fists. His ear drew closer to the door jamb.

'Not really,' she was saying with a soft, intimate laugh. 'I was just wondering if you'd done anything about the money?'

There was a pause, Gale heard the blurred sounds of Spencer's voice from the receiver, but it was impossible to hear what the other was saying. A wave of Dolores' perfume came to him as he stood there, tensed and sweating a little. He could feel the sweat beads along his upper lip.

'You were coming round to talk about that?' Dolores said. 'Tonight?' There was a thoughtful silence before she said: 'If you really want, but you'd better make it later.' Another pause. 'No, later than that. I've got a heavy date here. A little business deal, darling. It should yield a little of that capital we could use. Of course, darling. You know I do.' There were kissing sounds, and then the click as she hung up.

Why hadn't he put two and two together right from the start? He knew Dolores had brought Spencer with her; it should have been obvious to him when Miss Frayle had mentioned Spencer's noticeable absence from the party what had he been up to. Dolores and Spencer had worked the whole thing together. Somewhere one or the other had the swag and were now planning its disposal, whether to Lang or someone else was immaterial.

He had stumbled on the truth, and he realized suddenly, it looked as if he had solved his own problem in the nick of time. Much as he hated her, as low as Dolores had sunk in his estimation, wasn't there some compensation in his discovery? He could get back what he'd lost on his own, without the assistance of Dr. Morelle, without the risk of the police being let in on it.

Gale relaxed against the wall, holding his breath as he heard Dolores move across the room. He heard the sound of a drink being poured out. Then there was the striking of a match and he heard her inhale deeply.

Gale wondered who the business appointment was. Who was it who was going to provide her with the capital she'd referred to over the phone? Careful as he was to peer into the room, she hadn't once come into his eye line.

He braced himself to go in and face her. It would be a small consolation to shake her composure when he confronted her. He took a pace forward, but was stopped abruptly by the ring of the doorbell. He waited again, cramming as close to the opening as he could, and heard Dolores put her glass on the table and go to the front door.

He heard her greet somebody and the click of the door closing. Then the visitor was in the room. It was a man. It was no one that Gale could recognize by the voice.

'So nice to see you again,' Dolores was saying. But now to Gale's ears her seductive tone sounded mechanical, like a gramophone record that was wearing out. 'Do park and have a drink.'

'I haven't come here for a drink.'

Gale was startled by the venomous edge in the voice. The words were forced out as though through tightly clenched teeth. Dolores' visitor was tense as a fiddle string, fighting a losing battle with himself in an attempt to cover his jitteriness. Dolores, on the other hand, seemed typically calm and relaxed. Her voice was soft and persuasive.

'Don't act melodramatic, darling,' she said. 'I'm not going to bite you. And you know you don't have to do what I want. Though you were only too anxious to do anything I wanted. But that was when you really cared for me.'

'You've fooled me and cheated me from the day I first had the misfortune to meet you,' the man said. 'You're a bitch out of Hell.'

He moved momentarily into the fissure of light that was Gale's view of the room. Gale had time enough to see that he was a man in his fifties. A well-cut suit draped loosely over an ample figure; grey-haired and a face that was lined and drawn, heavy jowls. Gale had no idea who the man was.

'Take it easy, darling,' Dolores was saying. 'You've had your fun. All you have to do now is pay the price. I'm only holding out for what's due to someone who's given you her all.'

There was a sudden thud of a blow. Gale thought it was Dolores who had been at the receiving end, he heard her gasp as she collided with a table or chair and he thought she must have fallen. Gale hoped he was going to enjoy this, the prospect of Dolores getting a beating-up appealed to him, but her voice quickly disappointed him.

'Your wife should be thrilled to know how you treat a defenceless girl.' Her voice was still soft and insinuating.

The man muttered incoherently. There was another rush and crash of overturned furniture, then suddenly something heavy sprawled against the door and Gale rocked back on his heels as it slammed shut in his face.

'Keep your hands off me,' Gale heard Dolores gasp. 'Or it'll be the worse for you.'

Then the man's voice, breathy and choked with hatred. 'What do you want this time? How much is it? It's the last payment you'll get.'

Dolores' reply was lost. She and the man had moved away, and Gale couldn't hear what followed. He wiped the sweat from his face with the back of his hand, as he realized the black evil of the woman on the other side of the door.

CHAPTER TWENTY-ONE

The mustard-yellow Duesenberg 1934 model SJ super-charged convertible Riviera phaeton purred throatily down Harley Street, turned into Wigmore Street, and headed towards Baker Street.

Dr. Morelle had the hood lowered as usual, and Miss Frayle, sitting beside him, leaned back comfortably enjoying the freshness of the light breeze that had sprung up with the approach of night. Dr. Morelle got the green light at Marylebone Lane and the three hundred and twenty h.p. engine throbbed powerfully as he pressed his foot on the accelerator.

Beyond Edgware Road the soft red glow of the setting sun that had sunk in the West still brightened the evening sky. Miss Frayle blinked behind her horn-rimmed glasses, and raised a hand to shield her eyes from the glare that glinted along the rakish bonnet that stretched in front of her and caught at the windscreen.

At Marble Arch the Duesenberg swung through Cumberland Gate and joined the stream of traffic proceeding along East Carriage Road through Hyde Park. Park Lane ran parallel on the left and Miss Frayle glanced at the towering shape of Grosvenor House as they passed. Then the Dorchester Hotel, and Miss Frayle had a mental picture of distinguished men in evening dress and svelte, lovely women dining and dancing to the music in the restaurant whose canopied windows overlooked the Park.

As they approached Hyde Park Corner Dr. Morelle swung right along the carriage road which ran parallel with

Knightsbridge beyond the tall railings, past the back of Hyde Park Hotel, the lights of its restaurant gleaming through the trees, then the great red mass that was Knightsbridge Barracks with its great archway, to Prince of Wales Gate.

Dr. Morelle waited for the lights and then crossed over Knightsbridge to the top of Ennismore Gardens which faced them. The Duesenberg purred down the wide road with massive buildings on the right and a row of houses, tall and with pillared porticos, running along the left.

The buildings on the left gave place to a large square which was Ennismore Gardens itself. The Square was thick with trees and hedges, green and glistening under the light of the old-fashioned lamp posts.

The Duesenberg proceeded along the south side of the square, overlooked by great houses with wide porticos and balconies, at the end of which lay Ennismore Gardens Mews. Miss Frayle caught a glimpse of the old pillared archway which led into the mews before Dr. Morelle swung left into Ennismore Street. This was a narrow street with a high wall on the right and picturesque small houses on the left.

On past Ennismore Street Mews, with its cobbled street, at the end of which Miss Frayle saw a strange-looking clock tower pointing like a finger at the evening sky. They passed a house which looked like the side of a ship with portholes for windows, and beyond it an ornamental wrought-iron gate opening into a tiny garden.

Past Rutland Mews East on their right, and then Dr. Morelle slowed the car at the corner of a street which was Rutland Gate.

Ahead of them Ennismore Gardens terminated in a cul-de-sac, with a No Through Road sign prominently displayed. Dr. Morelle got out of the car and with Miss Frayle beside him, crossed over to a small opening in the high wall from which three steps led into Rutland Street.

The last light of the evening was beginning to fade, so that now a dusky haze obscured the pale gleam of the sky. Already a star was beginning to twinkle here and there. The neighbourhood seemed to be enclosed on all sides by tall houses and blocks of flats which backed on to the little streets and mews. In the windows of these houses lights began to glow against the oncoming night.

A little way along Rutland Street, Dr. Morelle turned right into Montpelier Walk, which was a collection of small houses and lock-up garages. Some of the houses were brightly painted and attractive, others appeared neglected.

There was a strange stillness in the air, broken only by a burst of laughter from a little public house which they had passed. They crossed the top of Fairhold Street and came into Cheval Place. There were several antique dealers' premises on their left, and shadowy alleys. Facing them loomed the dome of Brompton Oratory silhouetted against the darkening sky. They went along Cheval Place, at the end of which they turned sharp right, and found themselves in a concealed opening to a builders' yard.

This was Cheval Mews. An old motor van was parked on their left, and as Dr. Morelle, followed by Miss Frayle, entered the yard, a cat suddenly shot from underneath the van, paused to stare at them for a wide-eyed moment, and then disappeared under the door of the garage.

Beyond where a builder's and decorator's sign hung they saw a short flight of wooden steps, the balustrade of which was painted a brilliant blue. On the upright at the bottom of the balustrade was a crudely painted number six.

'This looks like it,' Miss Frayle said.

Involuntarily she gave a little shiver as if some chill in the atmosphere had struck at her. The silence was positively uncanny; the yard appeared completely deserted, and the shadows seemed to have fallen more quickly here than the rest of the neighbourhood which they had traversed.

Number six appeared to be the only mews flat; the rest of the buildings had been given over to builders, or remained in disuse. In one corner some upper windows had been broken and gaped drearily on the scene.

Dr. Morelle's sword stick echoed eerily as he led the way to the wooden steps with the bright blue balustrade. Miss Frayle glanced up at the windows, which were curtained with net. No light came from them. There was no indication that anyone was at home.

She followed Dr. Morelle, who went up the steps purposefully, until they stood on the platform outside the brilliant blue front door. Still there was no sound within of anyone stirring. Again that little shiver struck Miss Frayle, so that she drew the light woollen stole more closely about her shoulders. She glanced up at Dr. Morelle's saturnine features, shaded by the brim of his black hat.

'Do you think she's here?' Miss Frayle said. 'There doesn't seem to be a sound.'

'That we shall learn in a moment,' Dr. Morelle said, and pressed his finger upon the bell button.

Miss Frayle stared across at the darkened windows. She wished Dr. Morelle had sought his interview with this Dolores del Robia creature in broad daylight. The falling darkness seemed to give their surroundings a sinister, unreal atmosphere which, while common sense told her was nothing more than fancy, yet in such a place and at such a time common sense was so easily submerged by foolish fears. If only Dr. Morelle had not had to attend that scientific conference during the afternoon, this meeting which he seemed to think was so important with Dolores del Robia would have been over and done with hours ago.

Now they were kicking their heels in these unpleasant surroundings, for it was obvious the place was deserted. No lights burned. No response to the bell. Even the shrill tone of it sounded strangely loud and uncanny.

Miss Frayle stared at Dr. Morelle unhappily. 'The bell sounds very loud.'

Dr. Morelle nodded. 'Didn't you notice,' he said. 'The door is ajar.'

'Dr. Morelle,' Miss Frayle said quietly. 'I don't like this. I don't like it a bit.' She caught her breath. 'A stolen relic, dark sinister young women, flats with their doors half-open—and we haven't seen the worst.'

She wanted to get away. She didn't like it here at all.

'Stop trying to scare yourself, Miss Frayle,' Dr. Morelle said coldly. He pushed at the door gently with his sword stick and it swung back slowly on its hinges with a faint creak.

Miss Frayle hung fire.

'You first,' she said.

Dr. Morelle went in and Miss Frayle moved quickly forward to get as closely behind him as she could.

'It's so dark,' she whispered, her eyes seeing nothing but the vague shape of a room. 'Anyone at home?' she called.

The silence seemed to close in even more heavily as soon as her tremulous voice died.

'Dr. Morelle, I'm scared. Let's go away.' Miss Frayle's words came jerkily through chattering teeth.

'You don't really expect me to, do you?'

'No.'

He had turned to the wall close to the door. He snapped on the light switch, and the room was bathed in a soft pink light.

'Hmm,' Miss Frayle muttered, glancing at the furnishings. 'Nicely got up. Very arty and—' She broke off with a gasp. 'Dr. Morelle—over there, a leg—sticking out—'

A couple of swift strides took Dr. Morelle to the back of the settee. He stared down at the crumpled shape. Long, lustrous black hair covered the face, but even before he saw the white silk scarf twisted tightly round her neck, Dr. Morelle knew that the woman he had come to talk to would not answer any questions now.

CHAPTER TWENTY-TWO

Miss Frayle would have kept perfectly still if she hadn't been trembling all over. Her limbs refused to obey the impulse that urged her to step as far as the settee. She stared wide-eyed at the grim, impassive mask that was Dr. Morelle's face as he straightened up from viewing what Miss Frayle knew without looking was Dolores del Robia's dead body.

'I knew we shouldn't have come in,' she managed to say.

'If you feel faint, Miss Frayle, sit down and think of something nice,' Dr. Morelle said.

Miss Frayle forced herself to move, she stood back to the wall against which she leaned, carefully keeping the settee between her and what lay behind it.

Dr. Morelle touched one end of the scarf, both of which had been pulled so hard that the silk was twisted and narrowed from its original width; something about the scarf end attracted his scrutiny, then he crossed to the telephone. Lifting it carefully off its cradle by the base of the mouthpiece, he began to dial. Miss Frayle heard him say: 'Put me through to Inspector Hood.'

Miss Frayle remained against the wall, her gaze wandering from Dr. Morelle to the end of the settee where that leg reminded her of a wax figure in a dress shop window, and back to Dr. Morelle. It seemed that Inspector Hood was unavailable and another police officer was taking the call. Explaining the situation and giving the address, Dr. Morelle rang off.

'Hood is out at the moment. Meantime another officer is on his way, plus police surgeon, photographer, and the usual people.' His eyes flickered over Miss Frayle. 'We shall have to wait.' Absently, he moved a chair towards her. She sat down gratefully, her back to the settee.

Dr. Morelle went back to the telephone and dialled another number.

'Who now?' Miss Frayle said, her voice still shaky.

'Vere Spencer.'

Miss Frayle gulped. 'Do you think he—he—did it?'

'We intended calling on him after our interview here,' Dr. Morelle said noncommittally. 'He doesn't appear to answer.' He hung up and stood for a moment gazing intently at the settee. 'As soon as the police take over, we'll make that call on Mr. Spencer, Miss Frayle. No doubt you'll be glad to get out of here.'

'You've no idea how glad,' Miss Frayle said.

Dr. Morelle moved the cushion that had attracted his attention. The open flap of a thick manila envelope protruded between the cushion and the back of the settee. He pulled out the envelope which crackled under his touch. He glanced inside and then put the envelope in his pocket.

Miss Frayle had turned, hearing the sharp crackling sound, and watched him curiously. 'What was that?'

Dr. Morelle made no reply. Miss Frayle knew that he was in no mood to enlarge on the matter further, and she resigned herself to awaiting the arrival of the police, while Dr. Morelle went carefully round the flat.

Dr. Morelle had given the place a thorough once-over by the time the police arrived and went into their routine. He explained to the detective in charge—Inspector Hood had still not returned to his Scotland Yard office—how he came to be in the flat and discovered the body. He was, of course, well-known to the detective, whom he had met on several previous occasions, and he and Miss Frayle left Cheval Mews and went back to the car.

Vere Spencer lived in a small house in Chelsea. Dr. Morelle brought the Duesenberg to a stop outside a Georgian-type house at the end of a terrace of similar houses. There was a narrow alley, Miss Frayle noticed, between it and a warehouse-looking building. It had probably once been a tradesmen's entrance serving the back of the terrace. There was a narrow fringe of garden separating the house from the pavement.

Dr. Morelle led the way to the front door and rang the bell.

'There's no light in the windows,' said Miss Frayle. 'Oh, dear, I seem to have said that before. Dr. Morelle—'

'Calm yourself, Miss Frayle,' Dr. Morelle said. There was no reply to his ring and presently he stood back and glanced up at the house, dark and silent. Then he turned to her purposefully. 'Let's go in,' he said.

'Go in,' Miss Frayle sounded shocked. 'But the door's locked. Not like the other one—' Her voice faltered as a flood of memories swept through her.

'There should be a side entrance.'

Miss Frayle followed Dr. Morelle into the gloom of the narrow side alley into a small shadowy garden. A concrete terrace ran along the back of the house and dividing this from the patch of lawn was a cluster of untidy shrubs. It would have been fairly dark had it not been for the lighted windows of the building which formed the boundary at the end of the garden. It looked like the side of a dance hall; faint strains of dance music reached them, and moving figures were constantly silhouetted against the bright lights within.

Dr. Morelle tried the handle of the back door. It was locked. Next to it was a small sash window. Looking in, Miss Frayle could see it was a kitchen. A sink glimmered directly under the window, and on the further side she could make out a gas cooker. Dr. Morelle pushed the window so that it rattled. He observed that the catch was loose.

With round eyes Miss Frayle watched him take a penknife from an inside pocket, and insert it where the top and bottom frame joined. In a few seconds he had pushed back the catch and raised the lower sash.

'Dr. Morelle,' Miss Frayle said wonderingly, 'what are you going to do?'

'There are moments,' he said, 'when unconventional methods need to be employed when considering a given situation. This is such a moment.'

'You mean you're going to break in?'

'You are, Miss Frayle,' he said, invitingly. 'You're more agile than I.'

'Me?' Miss Frayle gasped. 'You want me to climb—in there?'

'I'll help you up,' Dr. Morelle said.

'But—?'

'It's a simple enough exercise to one of your slight physique.' Dr. Morelle's low voice was edged with impatience. He waved a hand negligently. 'You see that the door is adjacent to the window. As soon as you are inside you will find that there is only a key to turn, or a bolt to draw.'

Not without some initial reluctance, Miss Frayle allowed Dr. Morelle to lift her so that she could kneel on the window sill. She quite enjoyed that part of it, though Dr. Morelle muttered irritably when she clung to him convulsively at one moment when she felt she was slipping and in danger of falling off her narrow perch. Of course, as usual, he was right. Once she was through the window and had overcome a certain difficulty getting out of the sink, which was a trifle damp and slippery underfoot, only a few steps took her to the back door. A key was in the lock and she had the door open, and the whole operation had taken less than a couple of minutes.

Dr. Morelle closed the door after him and switched on the light. Another door opposite opened into a passage that led to the front of the house, and halfway along this was another door. Dr. Morelle opened this, and in the light of a standard lamp, which switched on from the door, they saw a smallish oak-panelled room furnished with an antique writing desk, a cabinet, some very expensive-looking chairs, and bookshelves.

'Looks like he isn't doing so badly out of the book-borrowing business,' Miss Frayle said. Dr. Morelle made no reply, he was gazing round the room with a speculative expression.

'No dead body, anyway,' she said, 'thank goodness.'

'Not yet,' Dr. Morelle said, his glance still travelling over the panelled walls. 'Tell me, Miss Frayle, where would you hide a valuable prize such as the volume which was stolen from Edwin Gale?'

Miss Frayle stared at him. So this was what it was all about? He believed that Gale's precious logbook was here, in this house in Chelsea. It suddenly occurred to her what this implied. That Vere Spencer had taken it away from that other flat, that one in the deserted, sinister mews in Cheval Place. More than that, it struck her with sudden, chilling force that Vere Spencer had murdered his accomplice, Dolores del Robia, in order to obtain the rich prize for himself.

Swallowing nervously, as these thoughts made their impact upon her mind, she turned to make some answer to Dr. Morelle. But he had forgotten her, his hooded eyes flickered over the bookshelves. She watched as he started to tap along the wall with the handle of his sword stick. 'Sounds solid enough,' he murmured, and she realized he was seeking some secret hiding place where Vere Spencer might have hidden the stolen property. 'What are you doing, Miss Frayle?'

Miss Frayle had promptly begun to busy herself at the writing desk, opening drawers and turning over their contents with nervous fingers. 'He might have just put it in here,' she said.

'Let me know when you find it,' Dr. Morelle said, and she thought she caught a sarcastic edge in his voice, as he continued his progress round the panelling.

'We aren't even sure it's here at all,' said Miss Frayle.

'If, in fact, it is in his possession,' Dr. Morelle said, 'we have to postulate two possibilities. One, that he has carefully secreted it from any prying eye. Or, that he had been careless enough to leave it in the most obvious place. Whichever it is must be a matter of mere speculation at this stage.'

'Dr. Morelle,' she spoke suddenly, and he turned to see her staring down into a drawer of the writing desk. 'See if you see what I see.'

He was beside her, as she lifted out a musty-smelling, tattered-looking oblong object. She opened the dark, worn leather cover to disclose a yellow, mottled page and read: 'The Logbook of Christopher Columbus. August 1492—October 1492.'

Without a word Dr. Morelle took it from her and thumbed through the tattered pages.

'It looks terribly old,' Miss Frayle said. 'I suppose it's a marvellous antique and all that, but imagine anyone paying twenty thousand pounds for it.'

Dr. Morelle seemed to be engrossed in the study of the faint, spidery script which covered the crinkled paper. It was only when there came a sudden movement behind them, that his head came up with a jerk, and Miss Frayle spun round towards the door with a little gasp.

Dr. Morelle slipped the book inside his coat and turned unhurriedly himself to face Vere Spencer who stood in the doorway.

He had a flat, ugly-looking automatic pistol in his hand and he was pointing it at them.

CHAPTER TWENTY-THREE

'Keep away from that desk,' Spencer said. 'And get your hands up. Both of you.'

Miss Frayle made a move forward. Spencer's gun swung on her, then with a shuddering moan she suddenly crumpled to the floor.

'What the—?' Spencer scowled at the inert figure.

'Give me a hand with her,' Dr. Morelle said. He bent over Miss Frayle, and Spencer lowered his automatic and came closer to help lift the limp form into a chair. As he did so, there came a swift, unexpected movement from Dr. Morelle, and Vere Spencer found his arm twisted agonizingly behind his back.

He let out a gasp of pain and dropped the gun. In the same movement Dr. Morelle scooped it up. The other stood there massaging his arm, his expression sullen, his mouth a bitter line.

Came a moan from the direction of the floor, and Dr. Morelle threw a swift glance down as Miss Frayle raised herself from a recumbent position. Her eyes behind her horn-rims, which had slipped askew, were wide open, and to Dr. Morelle's surprise they were smiling. As he backed towards her, the gun still menacing Vere Spencer, Miss Frayle jumped to her feet.

'It worked,' she said. 'And I never thought it did, except on the films.'

Dr. Morelle's glance was narrowed, as he placed himself in such a position that he could cover the glowering Vere Spencer with the gun, while at the same time give some attention to

Miss Frayle.

She was gazing triumphantly at Spencer, then turned to Dr. Morelle. 'Don't you think I'd make a good actress?' she said to him brightly.

'I must confess I was unaware that you possessed such histrionic powers,' Dr. Morelle said from the side of his mouth. His admission sounded reluctant, and Miss Frayle could not help smiling to herself with pleasure. Compliments from that quarter were rare.

'She was bluffing all the time,' Vere Spencer said, his mouth twisted. 'She hadn't fainted at all.'

'I know it was a rather mean trick,' Miss Frayle said.

'And I fell for it,' Vere Spencer said. He looked at Miss Frayle as if she was some insect that should be crushed underfoot.

'But after all,' she said, 'you had a gun. You might have killed us.' She glanced at Dr. Morelle inquiringly. 'He doesn't look half so dangerous now, does he?'

'It would seem that he had decided to cooperate,' Dr. Morelle said.

'I'm so glad,' Miss Frayle said. And she smiled encouragingly at Vere Spencer.

A look of understanding had crossed Spencer's face as he stared at them. 'You're Dr. Morelle,' he said. 'And she's your secretary.' His voice was peeved with an apprehensive undercurrent to it. 'You were at Edwin Gale's party last night.' His tone became charged with a desperate defiance. 'What the hell are you doing here, anyway?'

'All in good time,' Dr. Morelle said. 'Sit down and tell me why didn't you answer the telephone?'

'Or the doorbell?' said Miss Frayle.

'That was you who phoned, was it?' Spencer sat down. 'I didn't hear you at the front door. I was going to bed. If you must know, I've got one helluva hangover and I didn't want to be disturbed. Then I heard someone down here, so I had to come and see. I came prepared.' He glanced meaningly at the gun which Dr. Morelle held. 'What do you want?'

'Our mutual acquaintance, to whom you just referred, is wondering if you've finished with the book you borrowed from him. He'd like it back.'

Spencer looked blank. Dr. Morelle thought what a poor actor he was.

'I don't know what you're talking about,' Vere Spencer said.

'The Christopher Columbus Logbook is what I have in mind,' Dr. Morelle said. 'It was stolen from Edwin Gale's study while the party was in progress.'

'What's that to do with me?' Spencer said. 'I wasn't the only guest there. You were there, too.' He made an effort to force an unpleasant leer to his face. 'Remember?'

'Why how dare you—?' Miss Frayle's indignation was cut short by Dr. Morelle's almost gently-spoken reply, which nevertheless possessed a sting like a whiplash in it.

'But you happen to possess the stolen property.'

'Yes,' Miss Frayle said, 'perhaps you can explain that?'

Dr. Morelle took the leather-covered volume from his coat pocket.

Spencer stared at it, his mouth slightly open. Miss Frayle felt a fleeting sense of pity for him. Then she recalled the sight of Dolores del Robia as she had last seen her in the flat in Cheval Mews. Spencer made as if to move from his chair, but he checked himself as if suddenly resigned to the fact that he was beaten. He seemed to be having a fierce mental tussle with the question Dr. Morelle had put to him.

'What difference does it make?' he said at length. 'You've found the precious logbook and you're holding the gun. All the cards are stacked your way. Why don't you walk out with the loot?'

An icy smile flickered across Dr. Morelle's saturnine features. 'This is no longer a private problem,' he said, 'to be put right and forgotten. Other and unexpected developments make it necessary to probe more deeply. To inquire, for example, whether you or Miss del Robia were responsible for the theft.'

'Dolores?' Vere Spencer's face jerked up. 'What—what's she

got to do with it?'

'You know her.'

'So what? She was—' He broke off, his hands were trembling. 'What are you driving at?'

'You and she both planned together to rob Gale,' Dr. Morelle said with quiet remorselessness.

'You're out of your mind,' Spencer said wildly.

'After what happened tonight, at her flat in Cheval Mews?' Dr. Morelle said.

Spencer looked haggard, and Miss Frayle saw fear spread through every muscle of his tensed features.

'What—what happened? Tonight?'

'Let me put it this way,' Dr. Morelle said, his tone, biting. 'One of you stole this. It matters little which of you it was. Then, having achieved this first part of your plan, this evil woman determined to keep it herself. Perhaps she didn't trust you. You certainly didn't trust her. You went to her flat to get it tonight. She resisted—'

'It's a lie, A damned lie.' Spencer spat the words out. 'I didn't kill her—I didn't.' He slumped into a chair, sank his head in his hands. 'I found her like that. I didn't do it, I tell you. I swear to God I didn't.'

Dr. Morelle turned to Miss Frayle.

'He appears quite overcome.' With his other hand he handed her his cigarette case, and she took a cigarette from it and put it into Spencer's trembling fingers. He thrust it gratefully into a corner of his weak mouth, and waited while Miss Frayle lit it for him with Dr. Morelle's lighter.

Dr. Morelle returned lighter and cigarette case to his pocket, without taking a Le Sphinx for himself. 'Take a puff or two,' he said to Spencer, 'and relax.'

The other obeyed. He dragged at the cigarette as if he had been starved of tobacco for a long time.

He seemed a little better after a few moments but he couldn't look Dr. Morelle straight in the eyes.

'Let's get this business in its right perspective,' Dr. Morelle said. 'You went to her flat tonight and you say you found her dead.' He paused. 'Why didn't you get medical help?'

'I—I—panicked,' said Spencer. 'I didn't know what to do.'

Miss Frayle blinked and straightened her glasses.

'If she was dead, how did you get in?' she said.

'We knew each other pretty well. I had a key.'

Dr. Morelle glanced at Miss Frayle with a faintly sardonic expression, as if to warn her that she would be wiser not to interrupt with any of her own questions. Miss Frayle blushed and lowered her eyes. Then Dr. Morelle turned his attention to Vere Spencer.

'An innocent person would have telephoned for a doctor,' he said. 'You didn't. You didn't call the police. Could it be that you had something to hide?'

Spencer was breathing deeply. The cigarette wasn't helping him much now.

'I—I couldn't go to the police. You know I couldn't. It was this damned logbook.' He forced his gaze to meet Dr. Morelle's penetrating glance. 'You were right. I did go back for it. But I never intended to harm her. That's the truth.'

'When you got there you found she was in no state to raise any objection to your demand. You simply took the book and left? Is that what you would have me believe?'

'Yes,' Spencer said lifelessly.

'You and she planned this together,' he said, almost ruminatively. 'You deliberately stole the logbook from Gale, intending to sell it to the American, Lang. Then you found that neither of you could trust each other.'

'That's it,' Spencer said. 'I just didn't trust her to go fifty-fifty.'

'If she was already dead when you arrived, whom do you think might have been there before you? Someone else who was anxious to obtain the Columbus Logbook?'

'I don't know,' Spencer wiped his face with his hand. 'I don't know.' He suddenly sat up, staring across the room. 'But there was someone. Someone she was doing business with. I'd telephoned her earlier this evening to say I was going round. She told me to make it later because she'd got an appointment. Someone was coming to discuss a deal with her, she said.'

'You've no idea who?'

Vere Spencer shook his head. 'All I know,' he said, 'was that she was going to get something out of it. She needed money to get to the States. We were both going to try and scrape up the fare.'

'Why?'

'We'd decided it was the safest way to cash in,' Spencer said. 'We knew Lang was offering Gale plenty. We wouldn't make a deal with him here because of Gale. We thought it was worth following Lang to New York and clinching the deal there. We'd have spun him a yarn about Gale, and he wouldn't have been around to deny it.'

Dr. Morelle studied the dejected-looking figure before him through the haze of cigarette smoke that rose above the sunken head. Miss Frayle had the distinct feeling that, like herself, Dr. Morelle was impressed by Vere Spencer's story. There was a ring of truth in it. Looking at that good-looking, weak face, it seemed to her impossible that, rogue as he might be, he had murdered Dolores del Robia.

'You're in a tight corner,' Dr. Morelle said. 'You were at the dead woman's flat tonight. You took the prize which you and she had coveted, and stolen. She was your partner in crime and now she has been murdered. You say you found her body, but what evidence have you to support it?'

'I told you I panicked,' Spencer said. Beads of perspiration glistened on his forehead and ran down his face. 'And I was involved—but not with her death.'

Dr. Morelle might not have been listening. 'Furthermore, you had a motive,' he said.

'So probably had a lot of others,' the other said, with a desperate kind of snarl. 'Dolores was the sort who'd had it coming to her for a long time. And from a dozen different directions.' Spencer's expression grew defiant. 'And what about the business appointment? Maybe she double-crossed whoever it was and he took revenge. She double-crossed Gale. She was going to double-cross me. How do we know there weren't others?' His voice rose. 'I don't know who did it. All I know is, I didn't.'

It was then that a curious sensation overcame Miss Frayle. Vere Spencer's voice sounded far away. She shook her head in an attempt to clear away the mist that suddenly clouded her brain. But the effort only seemed to make her feel incredibly weak at the knees. She blinked rapidly, and made as if to take off her glasses, for they were suddenly steamed over, it seemed.

A horrible panic seized her. She was going to—no, she couldn't. She, who had put over such a convincing performance earlier, she couldn't really be going to—? Not now, it was too humiliating. She tried to pull herself together, but everything seemed to be slipping away from her. For some strange reason she seemed to be standing near a waterfall, at least there was a roaring sound like tumbling water in her ears.

She thought she could hear herself crying out aloud, but she couldn't be sure. Vere Spencer and Dr. Morelle suddenly began spinning round before her and then everything blacked out.

The impact of her hitting the floor brought Dr. Morelle's gaze round to her. It was only a split-second chance for Vere Spencer, but he took it. There was a flash of his speeding figure, then the slam of the front door closing after him.

Dr. Morelle had made no move. His tall, brooding shape towered over the crumpled figure at his feet. As he stared down at her, there was an unusual expression on his face. Though a sardonic smile touched the corner of his mouth, his hooded eyes held another look, it might have been of compassion, even a kind of reluctant affection. And then his face set again in the familiar gaunt lines, as he turned away from Miss Frayle. She had experienced a long and arduous day, he was ruminating, and the added excitement of the evening had proved too much for her. She was perfectly all right: the rest, enforced as it was, would prove beneficial to her. And slipping Vere Spencer's gun in his pocket he crossed swiftly to the telephone.

In a few moments he was through to Scotland Yard, talking incisively to Inspector Hood.

CHAPTER TWENTY-FOUR

At Oxford Circus Miss Frayle's attention was drawn to a news vendor at his pitch near the doorway of an office entrance, selling the midday editions of the evening papers.

"London Mews Murder," a contents bill announced starkly. Miss Frayle bought a paper. It was difficult among the jostling crowds to read properly the brief paragraphs which were boldly splashed across the front page. Miss Frayle tucked the newspaper under her arm alongside a batch of criminological papers in German and Italian, which she had just obtained from one of Dr. Morelle's colleagues, to whom they had been loaned. Miss Frayle crossed over and walked quickly up Regent Street towards Langham Place.

She turned into Margaret Street. A few moments later, in the comparative quietness of Cavendish Square, she paused and read the report.

It told her nothing she didn't already know. It merely stated that a certain Dolores del Robia had been found dead in her flat late the night before. The police, it said, wished to interview a man friend of the dead woman, whom they believed might be able to help them in their inquiries.

That was all.

Miss Frayle hurried towards Harley Street. She wondered where Vere Spencer was hiding himself, and whether Inspector Hood had yet run him to earth. What a fool he had been. If he was innocent of Dolores' murder, running away could only strengthen the case against him. His nerve had gone completely.

He couldn't face the police: he was obviously terrified that they would never believe his story. Yet she had the impression that Dr. Morelle did seem to believe it.

She found herself blushing slightly with mortification as she recalled how she had contributed towards his escape. It really had been ridiculous of her to faint away like that. Then she tried to console herself by reasoning that after all it had been quite an evening. She had felt such a fool when she'd come round, to find Dr. Morelle's sardonically amused glance bent upon her. She wasn't made of steel and whipcord. Dr. Morelle might be, but she wasn't.

Then she reminded herself that he always seemed to know all the answers to the puzzling questions in any case, yet they were kept locked up in that coldly calculating mind behind that gaunt, enigmatic face.

Last night, for instance. She thought back to when after he had telephoned Inspector Hood from Spencer's house, she and Dr. Morelle had gone to Mr. Reynold's flat in Bruton Street.

But he hadn't been there. His manservant told Dr. Morelle that Mr. Reynolds was away for the night.

Mrs. Reynolds? She was down at their house at Egham.

Where had Mr. Reynolds gone? The manservant didn't know, Mr. Reynolds had left no message. The manservant assumed that Mr. Reynolds was away on some business trip.

It was later, when she had returned with Dr. Morelle to Harley Street, and it was only after she had persisted with questions, that he had told her that Dolores del Robia had been blackmailing Mr. Reynolds. Which was why Dr. Morelle wanted to have a word with him.

Why couldn't he have told her this before, Miss Frayle couldn't think. And how much more could he tell her? Miss Frayle shrugged resignedly as she let herself into 221b. It was no use; Dr. Morelle wouldn't tell her anything until he was ready.

She went into the study and put the criminological papers on Dr. Morelle's desk. How he could think about them at such a time, when there was a dark and mysterious murder under his nose, she couldn't comprehend. She supposed it was typical of a nature which saw all occurrences dispassionately and objectively and never lost sight of every aspect of his work. She put the newspaper on the desk also, and was turning to go when Dr. Morelle came in from the laboratory.

'There's a bit about the murder,' she said.

Dr. Morelle glanced at the newspaper and then dropped it into the wastepaper basket.

'It tells the murderer very little,' he said with satisfaction.

'Surely that won't matter,' Miss Frayle said. 'Since he's the only one with all the answers.'

He bestowed upon her his pitying, thin smile.

'There is always information a criminal is glad to learn,' he said. 'He is forever anxious to discover how far the police are behind him. Which is, of course, why they take good care to tell him as little as they choose in the Press.'

'Have you heard from Inspector Hood yet?'

Dr. Morelle sat down in the swivel armchair behind his desk.

'He telephoned just after you'd gone this morning. He'd been trying to get in touch with Reynolds. He wasn't at his office or his home. I told him that was the information I'd discovered.'

'It's important he should be found,' Miss Frayle said. She thought she detected a grim shadow at the back of Dr. Morelle's gaze.

Dr. Morelle nodded.

'And Vere Spencer?'

The hooded eyes became narrowed. 'The police have had no success so far.' Dr. Morelle helped himself to a Le Sphinx. 'He's probably bolted to some hideout.' He flicked his cigarette lighter into flame and dragged deeply at his cigarette. For a long moment he studied the curl of tobacco wreathing upwards.

'Miss Frayle,' he said, 'telephone Curzon's Hotel and see if Mr. Lang is there.'

'Mr. Lang?' she said. 'Whom we met at Mr. Gale's flat the night before last?'

'I'd like to speak to him.'

'Of course.' And Miss Frayle quickly found the number and dialled.

Mr. Lang was in the hotel and after waiting a little while his quiet American accent came on the line.

'I'm speaking from Dr. Morelle's house in Harley Street,' Miss Frayle said. 'Would you hold on one moment, please? Dr. Morelle would like to speak to you.'

She handed the receiver to Dr. Morelle.

'We met the other night at the flat of a mutual acquaintance, Mr. Gale,' Dr. Morelle said.

'Sure, I remember,' was the enthusiastic response. 'It was a pleasure to meet you, Doctor. I was already aware of your great reputation.'

Miss Frayle caught the look in Dr. Morelle's chiselled aquiline features as the other continued in his flattering tone. She thought he reminded her of a sleek cat which had just devoured a succulent morsel. He was almost purring with gratification, she told herself.

'I was wondering if you might care to help me with a little problem?' Dr. Morelle said smoothly, his own voice pitched in a suitably flattering note.

'The idea that I can help you kind of takes my breath away,' Lang was obviously very pleased and intrigued at the request. 'But anything I can do, I guess I'll do willingly.'

'It is a somewhat urgent matter,' Dr. Morelle said, insinuatingly. 'I should like to discuss it with you reasonably soon.'

'Sure. I'd be delighted.' Lang paused for a moment. 'I've got to go out to a lunch date. How about directly afterwards, this afternoon? Say three o'clock?'

'That would suit me nicely.'

'Fine,' Lang said. 'See you then.'

Dr. Morelle hung up, and Miss Frayle saw the unmistakable glint of satisfaction in his eyes. She felt sure that he had settled some ingenious plan that would provide her with another mystery for her to wonder about. But she ignored the temptation to ask questions.

* * * * * * *

The yellow, rakish Duesenberg slid up outside the quietly distinguished entrance of Curzon's Hotel that afternoon, and Dr. Morelle's tall figure moved with raking strides into the foyer. The atmosphere was congenially discreet, the waiters moved cat-footed, their voices low and subservient. The clerk at the reception desk telephoned through to Mr. Lang's suite and two or three minutes later Dr. Morelle was taken up in the lift to the first floor.

The page boy escorted him along the first-floor, thickly-carpeted corridor to a door bearing a number five, and knocked gently. At Lang's invitation the pageboy opened the door and Dr. Morelle entered the quietly elegant sitting room.

Lang got up out of a deep armchair and took the Havana cigar out of his mouth.

'Delighted to see you again, Dr. Morelle,' he said.

'I'm glad to have this opportunity of renewing our brief acquaintance,' Dr. Morelle said.

The other indicated the armchair on the other side of the coffee table opposite his. He watched Dr. Morelle, who had refused his offer of a cigar, light a cigarette from his thin gold case. Then he drew at his cigar and settled back in his chair.

'You mentioned a problem, Dr. Morelle,' he said. 'Tell me what's on your mind, and how does it affect me?'

Dr. Morelle eyed the other for a moment, and then he said quietly: 'When are you due to return to America?'

The question took the American by surprise. He even had to think for a second or two, as if he found some difficulty in recalling the sailing date to mind.

'Why, next Wednesday, I guess,' he said.

'Would it inconvenience you if you changed the date to tomorrow instead?' Dr. Morelle said.

Lang sat up in his chair. He was frowning at Dr. Morelle with a puzzled stare.

'Tomorrow?' he said. 'I don't get it. What's the big idea?'

Dr. Morelle's enigmatic expression was lightened briefly with a thin, conspiratorial smile as he leaned forward and began talking persuasively, confidentially.

CHAPTER TWENTY-FIVE

Inspector Hood leisurely packed the blackened bowl of his pipe from the tattered old tobacco pouch and eyed the trim figure of Miss Frayle as she poured him a cup of tea. Despite the weighty problems that lay heavily on his mind, he could not help reflecting on how fortunate Dr. Morelle was to be endowed with such a discreet and efficient secretary.

She'd never babbled on like some women would have done when he'd told her about Reynolds. 'Poor man,' she had said, and her eyes had opened wide behind her horn-rim glasses, and he had the fleeting impression of a surprised schoolgirl behind the touch of makeup.

But she hadn't deluged him with questions. Neither had she answered any of his queries, except in an evasive way that was both polite and firm. He thought Dr. Morelle had trained her well.

'I really don't know what Dr. Morelle thinks, Inspector Hood,' she had said. 'His mind always works so far ahead of mine.'

Yes, Inspector Hood was thinking, she wasn't so naïve as she sometimes appeared. She was discreet. And as for efficiency, he glanced round the study. Its book-lined walls, its filing cabinets packed with neatly labelled dossiers and case books. The wide desk, uncluttered with papers, and everything in its place, the human skull which served as a cigarette box grinning up at him almost smugly.

Inspector Hood glanced at his watch. His heavy features

clouded a trifle impatiently. Of course, he'd called in at Harley Street without warning; he thought Dr. Morelle ought to be one of the first to know. Reynolds had consulted him.

Miss Frayle had caught the look the man from Scotland Yard had given his watch. She herself had expected Dr. Morelle's return by now. She was anxious for him to learn the news Inspector Hood had brought.

'I'm so sorry. Inspector,' she said. 'I felt sure Dr. Morelle would be back before this. You've already waited half an hour.'

'It's all right,' he said. 'You're looking after me very nicely, thanks.' He took an appreciative sip at his cup of tea. 'Besides, I'm anxious to see him. This new development concerning Reynolds closes the case as far as I can see. But I'm still a bit puzzled over this man Spencer. Of course, sheer panic and all that could account for his disappearance, but Dr. Morelle might be able to enlarge on his association with the del Robia woman.'

Miss Frayle nodded and glanced at the telephone, then at the clock on the desk. 'Shall I ring Curzon's Hotel,' she said, 'and if he's still there you could speak to him.'

Hood hesitated and drained his cup.

'Don't like to disturb him,' he said. 'Was it something important? I mean, d'you think it's anything to do with the case?'

'He went to see a Mr. Lang, an American,' Miss Frayle said. 'He didn't tell me why. But it's nothing whatever to do with that woman's murder.'

'Perhaps it might be an idea to ring,' Hood said, giving his watch another look. 'He may have left and be on his way back, in which case he won't be long. That old Duesenberg of his certainly gets a move on.'

Miss Frayle reached for the telephone. She had just begun to dial when they heard the front door. She returned the receiver to its cradle, and they both looked at the doorway as the gaunt figure of Dr. Morelle came in.

'Hope you haven't been waiting long, Inspector,' Dr. Morelle said. Miss Frayle fussed around him for a few moments and then passed him a cup of tea.

'Not at all,' Inspector Hood said. 'I dropped in on the off chance, I thought there was an item of news you ought to know about.'

Dr. Morelle glanced at him speculatively through the cloud of cigarette smoke from the Le Sphinx he had just lit. He wasn't misled for a moment by the other's elaborately casual manner. Inspector Hood hadn't dropped in while passing just to talk about the weather.

'Indeed?' Dr. Morelle's eyes narrowed. 'You've found Spencer?'

The Scotland Yard man shook his head. He looked at the bowl of his pipe. 'We've found Reynolds,' he said.

'Where?'

Inspector Hood didn't take his gaze off his pipe as he tapped some ash from it into an ashtray.

'In the river,' he said.

Miss Frayle was watching Dr. Morelle.

She felt pretty sure Inspector Hood's information must have shaken him as much as it had shaken her, when she'd first heard it. But there was no outward sign of his reaction. He leaned against his desk, looking at the detective with a probing gaze.

'Suicide?' he said at length.

'Undoubtedly,' Inspector Hood said. 'And I'd say for obvious reasons. He killed the woman and then went and did himself in. It adds up.' He paused. 'In spite of your advice, Dr. Morelle, advice he ought to have listened to, he had to go it alone. She put in the bite again, so he killed her. And who can blame him?' There was a moment's silence. A taxi sounded its horn ill-temperedly in Harley Street. 'Then he realized he was finished anyway,' Inspector Hood said, and stuck his pipe between his teeth.

Another long silence. Dr. Morelle appeared to be lost in thought, his mind far away. He might not have heard a single word that the other had spoken.

'He was unbalanced mentally,' he said, 'when he came to consult me. I was hopeful that he would give my advice its due weight and decide to leave the problem that was perplexing him to desperation in my hands.' He gave a sigh and shook his head. 'But her last demand upon him must have proved the final straw.' He eyed the Inspector levelly. 'Dolores del Robia surely drove him to do what he did.'

The telephone suddenly shrilled into the tense silence. Miss Frayle started. Inspector Hood wore an oddly dissatisfied expression on his heavy face. Miss Frayle blinked owlishly at the telephone.

'Aren't you going to answer it, Miss Frayle?' Dr. Morelle said.

'Oh—yes, of course.' She picked up the receiver. After a moment, she handed it to Dr. Morelle. 'It's for you, Doctor. Mr. Lang.'

Dr. Morelle gave a glance at Inspector Hood, and spoke into the phone. Then he said, after a pause. 'Perfect. I fancied he would be concerned. I'll get in touch with him within the next hour if he doesn't telephone me.'

Dr. Morelle replaced the receiver and a frosty smile lit up his enigmatic features. 'That,' he said, 'was someone I think you might care to meet, Inspector.'

Hood frowned at him and fidgeted his pipe stem between his teeth. 'Who is it?' he said. 'And why?'

'American named Lang. Quite an interesting individual, in his own quiet way.'

'I thought he was rather nice,' Miss Frayle said. 'Not at all the typical American, noisy and bright. More like an Englishman—you know, rather vague and self-effacing.'

'I know,' Dr. Morelle said.

'You mean there's a link between him and the murder? And Reynolds?'

'He was an acquaintance of Miss del Robia,' Dr. Morelle said.

'I don't quite know what's going on in that mind of yours, Dr. Morelle,' Hood said in a worried tone. 'Did this chap, Lang, know Reynolds, is that what you're getting at? Not that I can see it matters. I had ascertained from his manservant that he'd received a phone call from a woman early Wednesday evening and that soon after he went out. It's a certainty the woman was her.'

Dr. Morelle nodded, his manner was urbane and casual. But Miss Frayle thought she detected a triumphant glint at the back of his eyes, as if whatever activity he was engaged upon was going strictly according to plan.

'I advised you last night,' Dr. Morelle was saying, 'of what Spencer had told me before his escape, that Miss del Robia was expecting someone to call upon her in connection with a little business matter.'

'That was Reynolds,' Hood said firmly. 'And what more reasonable than that a man driven to murder should then be driven to suicide out of remorse? Reynolds was the type.'

Dr. Morelle said nothing, but bent and unlocked a drawer in his desk. Hood tapped his pipe stem against his thick knuckles and watched intently. 'Else why did he drown himself?' he said.

'He thought it was the only way out,' Dr. Morelle said over his shoulder as he straightened from the desk. Inspector Hood moved forward and stared at the thick buff envelope which Dr. Morelle had brought out of the drawer and from which he was now extracting wads of crisp five-pound notes. He pushed them and the envelope across the desk. 'Five hundred pounds,' he said.

Miss Frayle leaned forward.

'But that's what you found in the flat,' she said.

'Precisely,' Dr. Morelle said. 'I imagined it possible then that it was money Reynolds had given her. I removed it with the object of checking with him that night.' He eyed Inspector Hood who had looked up at him from the notes. 'When Spencer informed me of the woman's visitor on a business matter, it occurred to me that she might have been referring to Reynolds.'

'But if he'd gone to her flat with any intention of killing her,' the detective said sagely, 'he wouldn't have taken the money with him. And if he had killed her on the spur of the moment, he wouldn't have left the five hundred behind.'

'Of course he wouldn't,' Miss Frayle said, looking from Dr. Morelle to Inspector Hood who was wearing a somewhat deflated expression as he packed the notes back into the envelope. He pushed the envelope in his pocket, and clamped his teeth over his pipe stem, ignoring the fact that the bowl was cold.

'That was something which had not entirely escaped my notice,' Dr. Morelle said. And Miss Frayle was convinced there was a hint of mockery in his voice. If there was the Scotland Yard man affected not to notice it.

'If these are, in fact, his,' he said. 'Which brings us back to Vere Spencer again, and he's still at large.'

He looked at Dr. Morelle expectantly, waiting for him to agree or not. The tall figure had turned aside, the saturnine profile silhouetted against the window. Dr. Morelle said nothing.

'That scarf of his,' Inspector Hood said heavily, 'which the woman was strangled with seemed an obvious plant to throw suspicion on him. But perhaps we were being too clever. Perhaps it was him all the time.'

He looked at his black pipe bowl and puffed at the pipe impatiently. 'Unless,' he said dryly, and a match scraped and flared, 'you've got anyone else in mind, Doctor, we seem to be back at the beginning.'

Dr. Morelle permitted himself a faint smile.

'I am confident that you are nearer the climax of this business than you imagine,' he said. 'Why not come along to Curzon's Hotel, this evening, say, at six-thirty.'

'Where this chap Lang is staying?'

'Precisely,' Dr. Morelle said.

Inspector Hood pressed a large thumb upon the burnt tobacco in his pipe, and stared at Dr. Morelle. His expression of baffled surprise was almost as pronounced as Miss Frayle's.

'Curzon's Hotel,' he said. 'This evening?'

'Ask for Mr. Jonathan Lang,' Dr. Morelle said. 'You will be shown upstairs to his suite forthwith.'

'But—' Inspector Hood said, and then Dr. Morelle took him

by the arm and Miss Frayle watched them go out into the hall. She heard the front door open and close, and then the telephone woke into life. So that she gave a startled jump.

Her mind a seething chaos of questions and conjecture she pulled herself together and picked up the receiver. Dr. Morelle had heard the jangling of the telephone bell. He returned to his study to find Miss Frayle with the receiver in her hand.

'Mr. Gale,' she said.

Miss Frayle's thoughts filled with the image of the battered, travel-stained, leather-covered volume about which the man at the other end of the telephone had shown such desperate anxiety; was he aware that the precious object was now in Dr. Morelle's possession, and that it was about to be safely restored to him? But if she expected Dr. Morelle to betray any excitement or triumph at the prospect of being able to announce that he had succeeded in recovering the other's property, she was disappointed.

Without a word or any indication in his manner that he had any particular interest in the caller, he took the telephone receiver from her.

CHAPTER TWENTY-SIX

The rakish yellow Duesenberg turned into Half Moon Street, and under Dr. Morelle's expert hands inserted itself into a space between the line of cars in front of Curzon's Hotel.

Miss Frayle glanced in the driving mirror to smooth her hair which the warm evening breeze had disarranged. Her invariable routine after driving with the hood down, and Dr. Morelle always drove that way except in the depth of winter or when it was pouring with rain.

Dr. Morelle took the flat parcel from the dashboard shelf and waited for Miss Frayle to join him on the pavement.

They entered the quiet, almost somnolent atmosphere of the hotel foyer, Miss Frayle looking round expectantly. There were few people waiting about at this time. Mostly they were residents about to go in to dinner. Evidently Edwin Gale had been watching for them from a corner table. Miss Frayle suddenly spotted him as he got up from it and came eagerly towards them.

'Good evening to you both,' he said effusively. He wore an immaculately-cut dark suit with a dark, knitted tie. His face was smooth and smiling, his teeth agleam. 'I see you have it, Doctor.' He glanced at the flat parcel Dr. Morelle held. Looking at him more closely, Miss Frayle privately came to the conclusion that his face showed signs of strain. His eyes were a little red-rimmed as if he had been sleeping badly. The loss of the contents of the package Dr. Morelle carried had obviously given him a rough time.

'Mr. Lang's suite is on the first floor,' Gale was saying his manner expansive. 'After I phoned you I rang him. I explained you'd been able to recover the thing and that you'd arrange to meet me here with it. He was delighted. He said he hoped you'd come up, and see him again. He was thrilled meeting you.' He paused and smiled. 'I'd be glad if you would. You can better explain how lucky he is to be taking it back with him.'

He was urging Dr. Morelle and Miss Frayle towards the lift as he launched himself into a torrent of gratitude to Dr. Morelle for all that he had done in recovering his prize for him. As the lift purred upwards Dr. Morelle said:

'Have you been able to locate the other interested client?'

For a moment Gale looked a little puzzled, then his expression changed.

'You mean, the one abroad?' he said. 'No, as a matter of fact, I haven't. I've been too worried about the loss of the book to give him a thought, I'm afraid.' He shrugged faintly. 'Too bad for him,' he said. 'And it's too late now. I've decided, after all this panic, not to waste any more time, but to let the thing go while the going's good. Which is unlucky for this other character, but lucky for Lang.'

Dr. Morelle nodded understandingly. 'Incidentally,' he said, 'you'd better take this.' He handed the parcel to him as Gale knocked on the door.

Lang looked pleased to see them. Miss Frayle watched his eyes light up when he saw the parcel Edwin Gale was now carrying. The soft-spoken American pushed comfortable chairs into position, offered Gale a cigar which he took. Dr. Morelle smoked his inevitable Le Sphinx. Lang was smoking a cigar himself.

Miss Frayle gazed round the sumptuous sitting room, with its rich, if slightly old-fashioned-looking furnishings. There was a door almost opposite her. It was half-open and through the gap she could see the end of a wardrobe and a gilt cane chair. No doubt, she thought, the bedroom must be just as luxurious. All gilt and pink-shaded lamps, she felt. And there would be a private bathroom off it, with a sunk bath, of course. Her attention came back to rest on Edwin Gale.

He was unwrapping the book and she saw once again the battered leather, the crinkled edges of the pages yellowed with age. She noticed, too, Lang's expression as it fastened on the relic. Gale smiling at Lang, held it up as if for display.

'We are deeply indebted to Dr. Morelle,' Gale said. 'Had he not found the thief and recovered this, you would be going back to America tomorrow a disappointed man, Mr. Lang, I'm sure.'

The American nodded agreement. Slowly he reached for the volume, which Gale with seeming reluctance, allowed him to take. Lang handled it with a loving care. 'Treasure from the past,' he murmured.

'I admit I feel quite a wrench letting it go,' Gale said, his voice vibrant with sincerity.

'It would appear that you will be amply compensated for your loss,' Dr. Morelle said drily.

'It will be something to console me,' Gale said. His face was smiling, but that strained look was in his eyes. 'All the same, it's going a long, long way away.'

Lang placed the object of his affectionate attention on the table and took a slip of paper from his pocket.

'My bearer cheque for the twenty thousand pounds,' he said.

Gale had difficulty in not grabbing the cheque from the table, where it lay between him and Lang. His impulse was to snatch it up and be gone. But the interview must take its course, the polite yak-yak must go on for a while. He mustn't appear hasty. Just the opposite. Cultivate the impression that he saw the whole thing as just another deal. He thought that Lang was eyeing him curiously, waiting for him to pick up the cheque.

Almost absently Gale picked up the coloured slip of paper which meant twenty thousand pounds to him, and no one in for any cut this time: J.K., to hell with him; and Dolores del Robia was dead, and to hell with her, too. He put the cheque casually into his inside pocket, barely glancing at it.

'One tiny thing I'm kind of worried about, I guess,' Lang said thoughtfully. 'But maybe this is where you can advise me, Dr.

Morelle?' His gaze shifted to the tall, motionless figure who had watched the proceedings without a word.

Miss Frayle looked at Dr. Morelle, waiting for him to say something, but he made no reply to the other. Lang continued.

'Mr. Gale told me,' he said, 'when I called him to say I was leaving first thing tomorrow that this had gotten itself stolen during the party, Wednesday night. One of the guests, it seems.' He glanced at Gale. 'Is that correct?'

'Yes,' Gale said quickly, a little puzzled to know what all this was about. 'And I'm almighty grateful to Dr. Morelle for getting it back. As I said before.'

'Sure,' said Lang, as he looked at Dr. Morelle again. He drew thoughtfully on his cigar, whose light airy smoke mingled with that from Edwin Gale's cigar and drifted in the warm air. 'We're all aware of what happened to another of your guests, Mr. Gale.' He swivelled his head to the other. 'Dolores del Robia. I knew her—it was through her that I had the pleasure of meeting you, after all—and I was very shocked, deeply shocked when I read about her tragic end. But what I'm driving at is this. Though I can't see how this,' he had turned back to Dr. Morelle, and now he indicated the antique-looking object on the table, 'being stolen can have anything to do with her death, is there a possibility that the police may think there is some tie-up? What I mean is, ought I to clear it with the police before I take it out of the country?'

'Since you come to mention it,' Dr. Morelle said, 'it will in fact be required by the police as evidence.'

'What?' Edwin Gale's voice was rasping, his fleshy face had become taut with wariness. He took his cigar out of his mouth.

'You don't really mean that, Doctor?' Lang said. It seemed apparent that he believed Dr. Morelle was joking.

'So Vere Spencer murdered her for it,' Gale said slowly, before Dr. Morelle could reply to the American. 'That was how he came to get hold of it.' His friendly bluish-grey eyes fastened themselves upon Dr. Morelle. 'You never mentioned anything about this last night over the telephone.'

'Didn't I?' Dr. Morelle said, through a cloud of cigarette smoke.

'All you told me was that you'd got it from him, and that he'd admitted stealing it.'

'I must have forgotten the other matter.'

Miss Frayle threw Dr. Morelle, whose expression was suave, a look of baffled surprise. Was it Vere Spencer after all whom he had decided was Dolores del Robia's murderer?

Last night, it had seemed to her, he had dismissed him as a suspect, at any rate that was the impression that she had received. She supposed she'd got it wrong again. Suddenly Miss Frayle sensed an electric tingling in the atmosphere, a tautness of the air that set her heart racing. She was experiencing a sensation with which she was not entirely unfamiliar. A feeling that something was going to happen. Something that was not particularly pleasant, and it was going to happen soon.

'This the same man the police are seeking in connection with the murder?'

It was Lang's quiet American accents that obtruded upon the stillness. Somewhere through the half-open window came the murmur of London's traffic from Piccadilly nosing its way to the theatres and restaurants of the metropolis. Dr. Morelle nodded.

'So he's not only a thief,' Lang said, 'but a strangler.' Miss Frayle's eyes widened. She could hear her heart pounding so loudly now that she felt it must be heard in the silence which once again had fallen upon the softly-illuminated room, heavy with the aroma of Havana cigars. Dr. Morelle was contemplating the tip of his cigarette and then he glanced up casually.

'I have no recollection,' he said, 'of it having been reported that she was strangled.'

Lang had his cigar poised halfway to his mouth. He lowered it without taking a pull at it, his expression was mild, his tone unruffled. 'I guess that's an idea I had, I don't know why,' he said. 'Maybe it was because I was reading of some other case back home where the killer did strangle some girl.'

His answer came convincingly enough, and Miss Frayle thought the tension in the room slackened. She took a deep breath as she noticed that Edwin Gale was patting the palms of his hands with a crisp white handkerchief which had been showing in the breast pocket of his dark suit.

Something impelled her to glance to Dr. Morelle. A sudden stillness about him. That brooding quality which so often, she knew, presaged a moment of action when he would swoop like some eagle unerringly upon its prey. It seemed to her that his gaze was abstractedly bent upon the movement of Gale's hand returning the handkerchief to his pocket.

'As it happens,' Dr. Morelle said, directing his attention to Lang, 'you are correct. The wretched woman was strangled. Rest assured that the perpetrator of the crime, though he happens to be at large at the moment, won't long remain so.'

'Did Spencer admit to you that he'd done it in order to get this?' Lang said.

Dr. Morelle raised one eyebrow questioningly. 'Vere Spencer admitted to me that he was in the woman's flat last night.'

'But, of course, denied he'd done it?'

Lang said, expelling a puff of cigar smoke.

'Naturally,' Dr. Morelle said.

'They always do,' Lang said. 'But I daresay he gave himself away.'

'There was his scarf, of course,' Dr. Morelle said.

'And his initials on it,' Edwin Gale said, and then stood holding his cigar, his mouth sagging open.

Dr. Morelle alone was not staring at him with a sudden intentness. Miss Frayle had moved forward with a sudden gasp as the words fell from Gale's lips. Lang's teeth had bitten into the end of his cigar as if he had uttered a silent exclamation. As for Gale himself, his plump face had turned a ghastly greenish colour. There was a gurgling sound in his throat as if he was trying to retrieve those five words which had there and then damned him out of hand.

CHAPTER TWENTY-SEVEN

'How did you know,' Dr. Morelle said, 'the scarf had his initials on it?' He spoke to the other still without looking at him.

Edwin Gale fought desperately to find his voice. There was a dreadful hunted look in his eyes, as they darted from side to side, seeking a way of escape from the trap whose iron jaws had suddenly closed in on him.

Then the room seemed to have become crowded, as the bedroom door behind Gale opened wide and Inspector Hood, followed by two plainclothes men, bore down upon him. Gale heard their approach and turned to make a run for it, but he was too late.

He began struggling and shouting, and it took the two detectives all their time to hold him. After a little while he just stood still in their grip and talked in a loud voice. It was as if he had been attacked by some brainstorm.

Through Edwin Gale's distracted brain rushed a phantasmagoria, mostly spinning round his visit to J.K. down at Cape Cod, from whence he had set out all unwittingly upon the venture which had promised so much only to plunge him to the very bottom of the abyss. He mouthed incoherently about the intriguing glimpse of the sun-tanned girl on the terrace; and the tale from the old whaler's logbook of the murderous hunting of the blackfish. And all the time his mouth felt as it had when he had come into the sitting room and confronted Dolores. The man who'd started beating her up had gone. She was still dazed and in a state of semi-collapse, but when she saw him and realized he'd been there all the time, she'd practically frothed at the mouth. She'd turned as vicious as a wildcat. When she went for him he had felt as if his mouth was full of blood, as he whipped the scarf round her neck and twisted it and pulled and twisted.

He was still talking loudly when they took him away. Apart from the vocalising, he went quietly enough.

Miss Frayle went to the window which overlooked Half Moon Street and saw the police car drive off with the smooth-faced man in his dark, nicely-cut suit, his mouth still working overtime. And at that moment she suddenly caught sight of a figure wearing his inevitable bowler hat and striped trousers, and carrying his umbrella. Miss Frayle saw him stare at Edwin Gale, she caught the intrigued expression on his face as he watched the police car drive off. She remembered how that morning at London Airport Jim Catchpole had said that he thought he knew Edwin Gale's face, when he had seen him following Dr. Morelle across the tarmac. She had been in too much of a rush then, she remembered, to pay any attention. And she promised herself she must give the *Leader* ace crime reporter a ring and find out if he had recalled if he had really seen Edwin Gale before, and if so, what the circumstances had been.

It was about an hour later when Dr. Morelle and Miss Frayle were back at 221b Harley Street. They had been accompanied by Inspector Hood. Now they were in the book-lined study, a whisky decanter, soda syphon and glasses glinted invitingly on a corner of Dr. Morelle's writing desk. Miss Frayle was pouring from the decanter into a glass.

'That'll do nicely, thank you, Miss Frayle,' Inspector Hood said to her.

'I'm sure you've had a long and tiring day,' Miss Frayle said.

The Scotland Yard man nodded and took his pipe out from between his teeth. 'It's been pretty hard going,' he said.

Miss Frayle turned to the soda syphon. 'Say when.'

Inspector Hood duly obliged and took the sparkling glass from her. 'Here's all the best, Dr. Morelle. And not for the first time in our association I want to thank you for all you've done.'

Dr. Morelle permitted himself a faint, deprecatory smile. Then: 'Miss Frayle,' he said. She turned to him questioningly. 'Inspector Hood is not alone in having suffered a long and somewhat arduous day.'

'I'm so sorry. Whisky?'

Dr. Morelle nodded, and Miss Frayle mixed him a whisky-and-soda. It was one of the rare occasions on which Dr. Morelle availed himself of alcoholic stimulation. But, she told herself, as he took the drink from her that this after all was quite an occasion, he'd certainly earned it.

'Aren't you forgetting yourself, Miss Frayle?' said Inspector Hood.

'I hardly ever,' Miss Frayle said, 'you know my vice is a nice cup of tea.'

Inspector Hood took a long gulp, muttered something about it hitting the spot, and then said: 'I've seen some of them cave in when they knew the game was up, but that chap just couldn't wait to get it off his chest. It was like putting on a long-playing record. He coughed up the whole story. If you ask me, I think he's definitely peculiar in the head.'

'All murderers are peculiar in the head,' said Miss Frayle, 'or they wouldn't be murderers. Dr. Morelle will tell you that.'

'I know, and I'd be out of business, and so would he,' Inspector Hood took another drink. 'But the way he went on didn't seem to fit in with his appearance. His clothes, his manner, they gave you the idea he was a shrewd business man. And yet there he was burbling on about some chap he called J.K. in America; and some rambling yarn about a woman named Jennie Somebody-Or-Other who'd bumped off a whole batch of people way back. In America, too.'

'All the same,' Miss Frayle said, 'he was cunning enough to use Vere Spencer's scarf.'

'He says he didn't realize it was his until afterwards,' Hood said. He turned to Dr. Morelle, 'But had you got onto him before he dropped that brick?'

Dr. Morelle nodded over his glass.

'A few moments before,' he said. 'When I observed him take out his handkerchief to wipe his hands. It brought to my mind something I'd noticed when I was with him on the plane as we landed at London Airport. It can be for some people a rather unpleasant moment, but he appeared perfectly composed, as we touched down. Then I noticed him dry his hands, which were perspiring with fear on his handkerchief.'

Inspector Hood and Miss Frayle were staring at him with rapt attention. The Scotland Yard man had set down his drink for a moment, and was putting the flame of a match to his pipe. The match burned his fingers and he put it out while he listened.

'When I observed him go through identically the same motion a little while ago,' Dr. Morelle was saying, 'I knew that he was perspiring with fear once more. What had induced that apprehension was the reference to the scarf with which he'd strangled his victim.'

'She paid a high enough price for double-crossing him,' Inspector Hood said heavily.

Miss Frayle shuddered. A memory of that protruding leg behind the settee in the Cheval Mews flat flooded her mind.

'In that moment of fear,' Dr. Morelle said, 'he let slip the guard upon his tongue.'

The telephone shrilled and Miss Frayle was glad to answer it. The sound helped to rid her thoughts of the film of dark violence that was running through them.

'It's for you, Inspector,' she said.

He took the receiver from her and spoke into the mouthpiece. After a few brief words he hung up. 'They've just picked up Spencer,' he said, 'at Dover, trying to swim the Channel, I suppose.' And he reached once more for his glass.

Miss Frayle had turned to Dr. Morelle.

'One thing I still don't understand, Doctor,' she said.

'What is that, my dear Miss Frayle?'

'How did you spot that blessed Christopher Columbus thing was a fake? It was so brilliantly done. So convincing, the time and trouble it must have taken. The detail, it was an absolute work of art. I had a good look at it, I couldn't see anything wrong.'

'Yes,' Inspector Hood said, 'whoever the crook was, he certainly did a first-class job.'

'Except,' Dr. Morelle said, 'for one unpardonable error, which completely ruined the whole effect.'

'You tell me,' Miss Frayle said.

'He wrote it in English,' Dr. Morelle said.

ABOUT THE AUTHOR

(1908-2006)

by Philip Harbottle

Born in July 1908 in Dudley, Worcestershire as Vivian Ernest Coltman-Allen, **Ernest Dudley** grew up in Cookham, Berkshire, where his father kept a hotel. Stanley Spencer lived next door, and was a friend of the family. Through Spencer's patrons, the hotel became a meeting place for artists and actors. Ivor Novello was a weekend fixture. The comedian and film star Jack Buchanan helped the young Ernest rehearse a song for an amateur concert.

At the age of seventeen Ernest left boarding school and joined a theatre company touring Shakespeare through provincial Ireland, in village halls and cowsheds. From this he graduated to the more upscale Charles Doran Company, and performed in proper theatres, paying its actors the munificent sum of £2 a week. For the rest of life he used and was known by his stage name of Ernest Dudley

Always one with an eye for the ladies, Ernest soon met and teamed up with his late wife, the celebrated actress Jane Grahame.

Jane came from a theatrical family: her stepfather was Ellie Norwood, famous silent film actor who played Sherlock Holmes on stage. Through these family connections, Ernest secured work in the West End, appearing with Charles Laughton and Fay Compton, amongst others. When the original production of Noel Coward's *PRIVATE LIVES* transferred to Broadway, it was he and his wife who were recruited to take over the Laurence Olivier and Gertrude Lawrence roles in the British touring production.

His wife regularly played leading roles in the stage plays of Edgar Wallace, and Ernest would later create for her the character of Miss Frayle, assistant to Dr. Morelle in his radio plays. Other actresses would later take over the role. Most notably Sylvia Sims. Amongst the actors who played the good Doctor was Cecil Parker.

In the 1930s and 1940s he worked regularly for the BBC. In July 1942 his famous detective character (modelled on the autocratic film actor Eric von Stronheim, who he had met in Paris in the 1930s) 'Dr. Morelle' made his radio debut on *MONDAY NIGHT AT EIGHT*. Dr. Morelle was a big hit with listeners, and engendered a long cycle of novels and short stories, a play and a film, and three series on radio. At around the same time, he launched another very successful radio programme, *THE ARMCHAIR DETECTIVE*, which ran for many years, and Ernest became known as "The BBC Armchair Detective." In this weekly programme he reviewed the best of the current releases of detective novels, dramatising a chapter from each. They included his dramatization of John Russell Fearn's 1947 novel *ONE REMAINED SEATED*, and it was this fact that would cause Fearn's biographer Philip Harbottle to seek Dudley out some fifty years later, to become his friend and agent. Notable amongst his many other radio credits is the fact that he was the first-ever radio jazz critic. In the 1950s he transferred to BBC television with an early audience participation programme, *Judge for Yourself.*

Back in the 1930s Ernest also ran a parallel career as a newspaper journalist, specialising and pioneering in show business gossip, working for a time with Val Guest, with whom he had also earlier worked as a film scriptwriter in the British "quota" studio system. Amongst his many newspaper 'scoops' was how he had collaborated with actor Fred Astaire in a London nightclub on the creation of a new dance-step.

All of which only gives the bare bones of an amazing career as, variously, an actor, sports correspondent, jazz critic, playwright, novelist, gossip columnist, screenwriter and crime reporter. Most amazing is the fact that he became a marathon runner at an age when other people were drawing their pensions and relaxing by the fireside, and competed in several New York Marathons, writing a best selling book on how he achieved his amazing feats, *RUN FOR YOUR LIFE*.

Apart from some fourteen Dr. Morelle books, Ernest also published during his lifetime a dozen other detective novels, mostly notably *THE HARASSED HERO* (1951) which was subsequently filmed. He also appeared with short stories in leading detective periodicals such as *John Creasey Mystery Magazine* and, in the U.S.A., *Ellery Queen Mystery Magazine*. In the 1960s, and the following decades, he became established as the author of a long series of "animal" books for children, including *RANGI*, the story of a Highland rescue dog, and *RUFUS: THE STORY OF A FOX*. Ernest has also written novelisations of a number of films, along with a range of best-selling non-fiction books on diverse subjects, most notably *CHANCE AND THE FIRE HORSES* (Harvill Press, 1972) bringing to life Victorian London and telling the story of a dog, famous at the time, called Chance, who became attached to the fire brigade, and a favourite of the Prince of Wales.

An expert and enthusiast on the exploits of Sherlock Holmes because of his wife's family connections, Ernest wrote a two-act stage play, *THE RETURN OF SHERLOCK HOLMES*, which was successfully staged and taken on tour in 1993, with Michael Cashman as Holmes.

In 2002 a US publisher, Wildside Press, began to reprint some of his best detective novels, including a number of 'Dr. Morelle' adventures, in print on demand paperback format, available online. In 2005, the leading English publishers of 'large print' editions, F. A. Thorpe, began featuring Ernest's detective novels, in their Linford Mystery series, including the

'Dr. Morelle' books. All fourteen Morelle titles were quickly reprinted, followed by a number of new posthumous short story collections compiled by his friend and agent Philip Harbottle. These contained several unpublished Morelle short stories discovered in the author's effects, plus novelizations of radio and stage scripts.

Ernest continued writing right up to the end of his life. His last novelette, 'The Beetle', featuring Edgar Allan Poe's famous detective Auguste Dupin, was based on an earlier play broadcast on BBC radio, entitled *The Flies of Isis*. The new story was accepted for a Canadian anthology of Poe's 'Dupin' stories, alongside pastiche stories by John Dickson Carr and Charles Dickens. Ernest was checking the proofs in hospital at the time of his death. The anthology was fated not to appear, but 'The Beetle' has now been included in his new posthumous detective story collection, *DEPARTMENT OF SPOOKS*.

He is survived by his only daughter, Susan Dudley-Allen, a resident of New York in the U.S.A., who is devotedly overseeing the restoration of an amazing literary career.

Lightning Source UK Ltd.
Milton Keynes UK
UKHW012046290419
341807UK00001B/128/P